Mary Elizabeth Braddon

Phantom Fortune

A Novel: Vol. II.

Mary Elizabeth Braddon

Phantom Fortune
A Novel: Vol. II.

ISBN/EAN: 9783337050047

Printed in Europe, USA, Canada, Australia, Japan

Cover: Foto ©Andreas Hilbeck / pixelio.de

More available books at **www.hansebooks.com**

PHANTOM FORTUNE

A Novel

BY THE AUTHOR OF

"LADY AUDLEY'S SECRET"

ETC. ETC. ETC.

In Three Volumes

VOL. II.

LONDON

JOHN AND ROBERT MAXWELL

MILTON HOUSE, SHOE LANE, FLEET STREET

1883

LONDON:
WILLIAM RIDER AND SON, PRINTERS.
BARTHOLOMEW CLOSE.

CONTENTS TO VOL. II.

PHANTOM FORTUNE

CHAPTER I.

THE OLD MAN ON THE FELL.

HAVING made up his mind to stay at Fellside until after Easter, Maulevrier settled down very quietly—for him. He rode a good deal, fished a little, looked after his dogs, played billiards, made a devout appearance in the big square pew at St. Oswald's on Sunday mornings, and behaved altogether as a reformed character. Even his grandmother was fain to admit that Maulevrier was improved, and that Mr. Hammond's influence upon him must be exercised for good and not for evil.

'I plunged awfully last year, and the year before that,' said Maulevrier, sitting at tea in her ladyship's morning room one afternoon about a week after his return, when she had expressed her gracious desire that the two young men should take tea with her.

Mary was in charge of the teapot and brass kettle, and looked as radiant and as fresh as a summer morning. A regular Gainsborough girl, Hammond called her, when he praised her to her brother; a true English beauty, unsophisticated, a little rustic, but full of youthful sweetness.

'You see I didn't know what a racing stable meant,' continued Maulevrier, mildly apologetic, 'in fact I thought it was an easy way for a nobleman to make as good a living as your City swells, with their soft goods or their Brummagem ware, a respectable trade for a gentleman to engage in. And it was only when I was half ruined that I began to understand the business; and as soon as I did understand it I made up my mind to get out of it; and I am happy to say that I sold the very last of my stud in February, and Tony Lumpkin is his own man again. So you may welcome the prodigal grandson, and order the fatted calf to be slain, grandmother!'

Lady Maulevrier stretched out her left hand to

him, and the young man bent over it and kissed it affectionately. He felt really touched by her misfortunes, and was fonder of her than he had ever been before. She had been somewhat hard with him in his boyhood, but she had always cared for his dignity, and protected his interests: and after all she was a noble old woman, a grandmother of whom a man might be justly proud. He thought of the painted harridans, the bare-shouldered skeletons, whom some of his young friends were obliged to own in the same capacity, and he was thankful that he could reverence his father's mother.

'That is the best news I have heard for a long time, Maulevrier,' said her ladyship graciously; 'better medicine for my nerves than any of Mr. Horton's preparations. If Mr. Hammond's advice has influenced you to get rid of your stable I am deeply grateful to Mr. Hammond.'

Hammond smiled as he sipped his tea, sitting close to Mary's tray, ready to fly to her assistance on the instant should the brazen kettle become troublesome. It had a threatening way of hissing and bubbling over its spirit lamp.

'Oh, you have no idea what a fellow Hammond is to lecture,' answered Maulevrier. 'He is a tremendous Radical, and he thinks that every young man in my position ought to be a reformer, and devote the greater part of his time and trouble to turning out the dirty corners of the world, upsetting those poor dear families who like to pig together in one room, ordering all the children off to school, marrying the fathers and mothers, thrusting himself between free labour and free beer, and interfering with the liberty of the subject in every direction.'

'All that may sound like Radicalism, but I think it is the true Conservatism, and that every young man ought to do as much, if he wants this timeworn old country to maintain its power and prosperity,' answered Lady Maulevrier, with an approving glance at John Hammond's thoughtful face.

'Right you are, grandmother,' returned Maulevrier, 'and I believe Hammond calls himself a Conservative, and means to vote with the Conservatives.'

Means to vote! An idle phrase, surely, thought her ladyship, where the young man's chance of getting into Parliament was so remote.

That afternoon tea in Lady Maulevrier's room was almost as cheerful as the tea-drinkings in the drawing-room, unrestrained by her ladyship's presence. She was pleased with her grandson's conduct, and was therefore inclined to be friendly to his friend. She could see an improvement in Mary, too. The girl was more feminine, more subdued, graver, sweeter; more · like that ideal woman of Wordsworth's, whose image embodies all that is purest and fairest in womanhood.

Mary had not forgotten that unlucky story about the fox hunt, and ever since Hammond's return she had been as it were on her best behaviour, refraining from her races with the terriers, and holding herself aloof from Maulevrier's masculine pursuits. She sheltered herself a good deal under the Fräulein's substantial wing, and took care never to intrude herself upon the amusements of her brother and his friend. She was not one of those young women who think a brother's presence an excuse for a perpetual *tête-à-tête* with a young man. Yet when Maulevrier came in quest of her, and entreated her to join them in a ramble, she was not too prudish to refuse the pleasure she so thoroughly enjoyed. But afternoon tea was her privileged hour—the time at which she wore her prettiest frock, and forgot to regret her inferiority to Lesbia in all the graces of womanhood.

One afternoon, when they had all three walked to Easedale Tarn, and were coming back by the side of the force, picking their way among the grey stones and the narrow threads of silvery water, it suddenly occurred to Hammond to ask Mary about that queer old man he had seen on the Fell nearly a fortnight before. He had often thought of making the inquiry when he was away from Mary, but had always forgotten the thing when he was with her. Indeed Mary had a wonderful knack of making him forget everything but herself.

'You seem to know every creature in Grasmere, down to the two-year-old babies,' said

Hammond, Mary having just stopped to converse with an infantine group, straggling and struggling over the boulders. 'Pray, do you happen to know a man called Barlow, a very old man?'

'Old Sam Barlow,' exclaimed Mary; 'why, of course I know him.'

She said it as if he were a near relative, and the question palpably absurd.

'He is an old man, a hundred, at least, I should think,' said Hammond.

'Poor old Sam, not much on the wrong side of eighty. I go to see him every week, and take him his week's tobacco, poor old dear. It is his only comfort.'

'Is it?' asked Hammond. 'I should have doubted his having so humanising a taste as tobacco. He looks too evil a creature ever to have yielded to the softening influence of a pipe.'

'An evil creature! What, old Sam? Why he is the most genial old thing, and as cheery —loves to hear the newspaper read to him— the murders and railway accidents. He doesn't care for politics. Everybody likes old Sam Barlow.'

'I fancy the Grasmere idea of reverend and amiable age must be strictly local. I can only say that I never saw a more unholy countenance.'

'You must have been dreaming when you saw him,' said Mary. 'Where did you meet him?'

'On the Fell, about a quarter of a mile from the shrubbery gate.'

'*Did* you? I shouldn't have thought he could have got so far. I've a good mind to take you to see him, this very afternoon, before we go home.'

'Do,' exclaimed Hammond, 'I should like it immensely. I thought him a hateful-looking old person; but there was something so thoroughly uncanny about him that he exercised an absolute fascination upon me; he magnetised me, I think, as the green-eyed cat magnetises the bird. I have been positively longing to see him again. He is a kind of human monster, and I hope some one will have a big bottle made ready for him and preserve him in spirits when he dies,'

'What a horrid idea! No, sir, dear old

Barlow shall lie beside the Rotha, under the trees
Wordsworth planted. He is such a man as Wordsworth would have loved.'

Mr. Hammond shrugged his shoulders, and
said no more. Mary's little vehement ways, her
enthusiasm, her love of that valley, which might
be called her native place, albeit her eyes had
opened upon heaven's light far away, her humility,
were all very delightful in their way. She was
not a perfect beauty, like Lesbia; but she was a
fresh pure-minded English girl, frank as the day,
and if he had had a brother he would have
recommended that brother to choose just such a girl
for his wife.

Mr. Samuel Barlow occupied a little old cottage,
which seemed to consist chiefly of a gable end
and a chimney stack, in that cluster of dwellings
behind St. Oswald's church, which was once
known as the Kirk Town. Visitors went downstairs to get to Mr. Barlow's ground-floor, for
the influence of time and advancing civilisation
had raised the pathway in front of Mr. Barlow's
cottage until his parlour had become of a cellar-

like aspect. Yet it was a very nice little parlour when one got down to it, and it enjoyed winter and summer a perpetual twilight, since the light that crept through the leaded casement was tempered by a screen of flowerpots, which were old Barlow's particular care. There were no finer geraniums in all Grasmere than Barlow's, no bigger carnations or picotees, asters or arums.

It was about five o'clock in the March afternoon, when Mary ushered John Hammond into Mr. Barlow's dwelling, and, in the dim glow of a cheery little fire and the faint light that filtered through the screen of geranium leaves, the visitor looked for a moment or so doubtfully at the owner of the cottage. But only for a moment. Those bright blue eyes and apple cheeks, that benevolent expression, bore no likeness to the strange old man he had seen on the Fell. Mr. Barlow was toothless and nut-cracker like of outline; he was thin and shrunken, and bent with the burden of long years; but his healthy visage had none of those deep lines, those cross markings and hollows which made the pallid countenance of that other old man as ghastly as would be the abstract idea of life's last stage embodied by the bitter pencil of a Hogarth.

'I have brought a gentleman from London to see you, Sam,' said Mary. 'He fancied he met you on the Fell the other morning.'

Barlow rose and quavered a cheery welcome, but protested against the idea of his having got so far as the Fell.

'With my blessed rheumatics, you know it isn't in me, Lady Mary. I shall never get no further than the churchyard; but I likes to sit on the wall hard by Wordsworth's tomb in a warm afternoon, and to see the folks pass over the bridge; and I can potter about looking after my flowers, I can. But it would be a dull life now the poor old missus is gone, and the bairns all out at service, if it wasn't for some one dropping in to have a chat, or read me a bit of the news sometimes. And there isn't anybody in Grasmere, gentle or simple, that's kinder to me than you, Lady Mary. Lord bless you, I do ·look forward to my newspaper. Any more of them dreadful smashes?'

'No Sam, thank Heaven, there have been no railway accidents.'

'Ah, we shall have 'em in August and September,' said the old man, cheerily. 'They're bound to come then. There's a time for all things, as Solomon says. When the season comes the smashes will come. And no more of these mysterious murders, I suppose, which baffle the police and keep me awake o' nights thinking of 'em.'

'Surely you do not take delight in murder, Mr. Barlow?' said Hammond.

'No, sir, I do not wish my fellow-creatures to make away with each other; but if there is a murder going in the papers I like to get the benefit of it. I like to sit in front of my fire of an evening and wonder about it while I smoke my pipe, and fancy I can see the murderer hiding in a garret in an out-of-the-way alley, or as a stowaway on board a big ship, or as a miner deep down in a coalpit, and never thinking that even there the police can track him. Did you ever hear of Mr. de Quincey, sir?'

'I believe I have read every line he ever wrote.'

'Ah, you should have heard him talk about murders. It would have made you dream queer dreams, just as he did. He lived for years in the white cottage that Wordsworth once lived in, just behind the street yonder—a nice neat little gentleman, in a houseful of books. I've had many a talk with him when I was a young man.'

' And how old may you be now,' Mr. Barlow ? '

' Getting on for eighty-four, sir.'

' But you are not the oldest man in Grasmere, I should say, by twenty years ? '

' I don't think there's many much older than me, sir.'

' The man I saw on the Fell looked at least a hundred. I wish you could tell me who he is; I feel a morbid curiosity about him.'

He went on to describe the old man in the grey coat, as minutely as he could, dwelling on every characteristic of that singular-looking old person ; but Samuel Barlow could not identify the description with any one in Grasmere. Yet a man of that age, seen walking on the hill-side at eight in the morning, could hardly have come from far afield.

CHAPTER II.

ALTHOUGH Maulevrier had assured his grandmother that John Hammond would take flight at the first warning of Lesbia's return, Lady Maulevrier's dread of any meeting between her granddaughter and that ineligible lover determined her in making such arrangements as should banish Lesbia from Fellside, so long as there seemed the slightest danger of such a meeting. She knew that Lesbia had loved her fortuneless suitor; and she did not know that the wound was cured, even by a season in the little-great world of Cannes. Now that she, the ruler of that household, was a helpless captive in her own apartments, she felt that Lesbia at Fellside would be her own mistress, and hemmed round with the dangers that beset richly-dowered beauty and inexperienced youth.

John Hammond might be playing a very deep game, perhaps assisted by Maulevrier. He might ostensibly leave Fellside before Lesbia's return, yet lurk in the neighbourhood, and contrive to meet her every day. If Maulevrier encouraged this folly, they might be married and over the border, before her ladyship—fettered, impotent as she was—could interfere.

Lady Maulevrier felt that Georgie Kirkbank was her strong rock. So long as Lesbia was under that astute veteran's wing there could be no danger. In that embodied essence of worldliness and diplomacy, there was an ever-present defence from all temptations that spring from romance and youthful impulses. It was a bitter thing, perhaps, to steep a young and pure soul in such an atmosphere, to harden a fresh young nature in the fiery crucible of fashionable life; but Lady Maulevrier believed that the end would sanctify the means. Lesbia, once married to a worthy man, such a man as Lord Hartfield, for instance, would soon rise to a higher level than that Belgravian swamp over which the malarian vapours of falsehood, and slander, and self-seeking, and prurient imaginings hang dense and thick. She would rise to the loftier table-land of that really great world which governs and admonishes the ruck of mankind by examples of noble deeds and noble thoughts; the world of statesmen, and soldiers, and thinkers, and reformers; the salt wherewithal society is salted.

But while Lesbia was treading the tortuous mazes of fashion, it was well for her to be guided and guarded by such an old campaigner as Lady Kirkbank, a woman who, in the language of her friends, 'knew the ropes.'

Lesbia's last letter had been to the effect that she was to go back to London with the Kirkbanks directly after Easter, and that directly they arrived she would set off with her maid for Fellside, to spend a week or a fortnight with her dearest grand-mother, before going back to Arlington Street for the May campaign.

'And then, dearest, I hope you will make up your mind to spend the season in London,' wrote Lesbia. 'I shall expect to hear that you have secured Lord Porlock's house. How dreadfully slow

your poor dear hand is to recover! I am afraid
Horton is not treating the case cleverly. Why do
you not send for Mr. Erichsen? It is a shock to
my nerves every time I receive a letter in Mary's
masculine hand, instead of in your lovely Italian
penmanship. Strange—isn't it?—how much better
the women of your time write than the girls of
the present day! Lady Kirkbank receives letters
from stylish girls in a hand that would disgrace
a housemaid.'

Lady Maulevrier allowed a post to go by before
she answered this letter, while she deliberated upon
the best and wisest manner of arranging her granddaughter's future. It was an agony to her not to be
able to write with her own hand, to be obliged to so
shape every sentence that Mary might learn nothing
which she ought not to know. It was impossible
with such an amanuensis to write confidentially
to Lady Kirkbank. The letters to Lesbia were of
less consequence; for Lesbia, albeit so intensely
beloved, was not in her grandmother's confidence,
least of all about those schemes and dreams
which concerned her own fate.

However, the letters had to be written, so Mary was told to open her desk and begin.

The letter to Lesbia ran thus :—

'My dearest Child,

'This is a world in which our brightest day-dreams generally end in mere dreaming. For years past I have cherished the hope of presenting you to your sovereign, to whom I was presented six and-forty years ago, when she was so fair and girlish a creature that she seemed to me more like a queen in a fairy tale than the actual ruler of a great country. I have beguiled my monotonous days with thoughts of the time when I should return to the great world, full of pride and delight in showing old friends what a sweet flower I had reared in my mountain home; but, alas, Lesbia, it may not·be.

'Fate has willed otherwise. The maimed hand does not recover, although Horton is very clever, and thoroughly understands my case. I am not ill, I am not in danger; so you need feel no anxiety about me; but I am a cripple; and I am likely to remain a cripple for months; so the idea of a London season this year is hopeless.

'Now, as you have in a manner made your *début* at Cannes, it would never do to bury you here for another year. You complained of the dulness last summer; but you would find Fellside much duller now that you have tasted the elixir of life. No, my dear love, it will be well for you to be presented, as Lady Kirkbank proposes, at the first drawing-room after Easter; and Lady Kirkbank will have to present you. She will be pleased to do this, I know, for her letters are full of enthusiasm about you. And, after all, I do not think you will lose by the exchange. Clever as I think myself, I fear I should find myself sorely at fault in the society of to-day. All things are changed: opinions, manners, creeds, morals even. Acts that were crimes in my day are now venial errors— opinions that were scandalous are now the mark of "advanced thought." I should be too formal for this easy-going age, should be ridiculed as old-fashioned and narrow-minded, should put you to the blush a dozen times a day by my prejudices and opinions.

'It is very good of you to think of travelling so long a distance to see me; and I should love to look at your sweet face, and hear you describe your new experiences; but I could not allow you to travel with only the protection of a maid; and there are many reasons why I think it better to defer the meeting till the end of the season, when Lady Kirkbank will bring my treasure back to me, eager to tell me the history of all the hearts she has broken.'

The dowager's letter to Lady Kirkbank was brief and business-like. She could only hope that her old friend Georgie, whose acuteness she knew of old, would divine her feelings and her wishes, without being explicitly told what they were.

'My dear Georgie,

'I am too ill to leave this house; indeed I doubt if I shall ever leave it till I am taken away in my coffin; but please say nothing to alarm Lesbia. Indeed, there is no ground for fear, as I am not dangerously ill, and may drag out an imprisonment of long years before the coffin comes to fetch me. There are reasons, which you will understand, why Lesbia should not come here till after the season; so please keep her in Arlington Street, and occupy her mind as much as you can with the preparations for her first campaign. I give you *carte blanche.* If Carson is still in business I should like her to make my girl's gowns; but you must please yourself in this matter, as it is quite possible that Carson is a little behind the times.

'I must ask you to present my darling, and to deal with her exactly as if she were a daughter of your own. I think you know all my views and hopes about her; and I feel that I can trust to your friendship in this my day of need. The dream of my life has been to launch her myself, and direct her every step in the mazes of town life; but that dream is over. I have kept age and infirmity at a distance, have even forgotten that the years were going by; and now I find myself an old woman all at once, and my golden dream has vanished.'

. Lady Kirkbank's reply came by return of post,

and happily this gushing epistle had not to be submitted to Mary's eye.

'My dearest Di,

'My heart positively bleeds for you, What *is* the matter with your hand, that you talk of being a life-long prisoner to your room? Pray send for Paget or Erichsen, and have yourself put right at once. No doubt that local simpleton is making a mess of your case. Perhaps while he is dabbling with lint and lotions the real remedy is the knife. I am sure amputation would be less melancholy than the despondent state of feeling which you are now suffering. If any limb of mine went wrong I should say to the surgeon, " Cut it off, and patch up the stump in your best style; I give you a fortnight, and at the end of that time I expect to be going to parties again." Life is not long enough for dawdling surgery.

'As regards Lesbia, I can only say that I adore her, and I am enchanted at the idea that I am to run her myself. I intend her to be *the* beauty of the season—not *one of the loveliest débutantes*, or any rot of that kind—but just the girl whom everybody will be crazy about. There shall be a mob wherever she appears, Di, I promise you that. There is no one in London who can work a thing of that kind better than your humble servant. And when once the girl is the talk of the town, all the rest is easy. She can choose for herself among the very best men in society. Offers will pour in as thickly as circulars from undertakers and mourning ware-houses, after a death.

'Lesbia is so cool-headed and sensible that I have not the least doubt of her success. With an impulsive or romantic girl there is always the fear of a *fiasco*. But this sweet child of yours has been well brought up, and knows her own value. She behaved like a queen here, where I need not tell you society is just a little mixed; though, of course, we only cultivate our own set. Your heart would swell with pride if you could see the way she puts down men who are not quite good style; and the ease with which she crushes those odious American girls, with their fine complexions and loud manners.

'Be assured that I shall guard her as the apple of my eye, and that the detrimental who circumvents me will be a very Satan of schemers.

'I can but smile at your mention of Carson, whose gowns used to fit us so well in our girlish days, and whose bills seem moderate compared with the exorbitant accounts I get now.

'Carson has long been forgotten, my dear soul, gone with the snows of last year. A long procession of fashionable French dressmakers has passed across the stage since her time, like the phantom kings in Macbeth ; and now the last rage is to have our gowns made by an Englishman who works for the Princess, and who gives himself most insufferable airs, or an Irishwoman who is employed by all the best actresses. It is to the latter, Kate Kearney, I shall entrust our sweet Lesbia's toilettes.'

The same post brought a loving letter from Lesbia, full of regret at not being allowed to go down to Fellside, and yet full of delight at the prospect of her first season.

'Lady Kirkbank and I have been discussing my court dress,' she wrote, 'and we have decided upon a white cut-velvet train, with a border of ostrich feathers, over a satin petticoat embroidered with seed pearl. It will be dear, but we know you will not mind that. Lady Kirkbank takes the idea from the costume Buckingham wore at the Louvre the first time he met Anne of Austria. Isn't that clever of her? She is not a deep thinker like you; is horribly ignorant of science, metaphysics, poetry even. She asked me one day who Plato was, and whether he took his name from the battle of Platœa; aud she says she never could understand why people make a fuss about Shakespeare; but she has read all the secret histories and memoirs that ever were written, and knows all the ins and outs of court life and high life for the last three hundred years; and there is not a person in the peerage whose family history she has not at her fingers' ends, except my grandfather. When I asked her to tell me all about Lord Maulevrier and his achievements as Governor of Madras, she had not a word to say. So, perhaps, she draws upon her invention a little in talking about other people, and felt herself restrained when she came to speak of my grandfather.'

This passage in Lesbia's letter affected Lady Maulevrier as if a scorpion had wriggled from underneath the sheet of paper. She folded the letter, and laid it in the satin-lined box on her table, with a deep sigh.

'Yes, she is in the world now, and she will ask questions. I have never warned her against pronouncing her grandfather's name. There are some who will not be so kind as Georgie Kirkbank; some, perhaps, who will delight in humiliating her, and who will tell her the worst that can be told. My only hope is that she will make a great marriage, and speedily. Once the wife of a man with a high place in the world, worldlings will be too wise to wound her by telling her that her grandfather was an unconvicted felon.'

The die was cast. Lady Maulevrier might

dread the hazard of evil tongues, of slanderous memories; but she could not recall her consent to Lesbia's *débul*. The girl was already launched; she had been seen and admired. The next stage in her career must be to be wooed and won by a worthy wooer.

CHAPTER III.

WHILE these plans were being settled, and while Lesbia's future was the all-absorbing subject of Lady Maulevrier's thoughts, Mary contrived to be happier than she had ever been in her life before. It was happiness that grew and strengthened with every day; and yet there was no obvious reason for this deep joy. Her life ran in the same familiar groove. She walked and rode on the old pathways; she rowed on the lake she had known from babyhood; she visited her cottagers, and taught in the village school, just the same as of old. The change was only that she was no longer alone; and of late the solitude of her life, the ever-present consciousness that nobody shared her pleasures or sympathised with her upon any point, had weighed upon her like an actual burden. Now she had Maulevrier, who was always kind, who understood and shared almost all her tastes, and Maulevrier's friend, who, although not given to saying smooth things, seemed warmly interested in her pursuits and opinions. He encouraged her to talk, although he generally took the opposite side in every argument; and she no longer felt oppressed or irritated by the idea that he despised her.

Indeed, although he never flattered or even praised her, Mr. Hammond let her see that he liked her society. She had gone out of her way to avoid him, very fearful lest he should think her bold or masculine; but he had taken pains to frustrate all her efforts in that direction; he had refused to go upon excursions which she could not share. 'Lady Mary must come with us,' he said, when they were planning a morning's ramble. Thus it happened that Mary was his guide and companion in all his walks, and roamed with him bamboo in hand, over every one of those mountainous paths she knew and loved so well.

Distance was as nothing to them — sometimes a boat helped them, and they went over wintry Windermere to climb the picturesque heights above Bowness. Sometimes they took ponies, and a groom, and left their steeds to perform the wilder part of the way on foot. In this wise John Hammond saw all that was to be seen within a day's journey of Grasmere, except the top of Helvellyn. Maulevrier had shirked the expedition, had always put off Mary and Mr. Hammond when they proposed it. The season was not advanced enough — the rugged pathway by the Tongue Ghyll would be as slippery as glass — no pony could get up there in such weather.

'We have not had any frost to speak of for the last fortnight,' pleaded Mary, who was particularly anxious to do the honours of Helvellyn, as the real lion of the neighbourhood.

'What a simpleton you are, Molly!' cried Maulevrier. 'Do you suppose because there is no frost in your grandmother's garden — and if you were to ask Staples about his peaches he would **tell** you a very **different** story — that there's a tropical atmosphere on Dolly Waggon Pike ? **Why,** I'd **wager** the ice **on** Grisdale Tarn **is** thick enough for skating. Helvellyn won't **run** away, child. **You and** Hammond can **dance the** Highland Schottische **on** Striding Edge **in June, if** you like.'

'Mr. Hammond won't be here in June,' said Mary.

'Who knows ?—the **train** service is pretty fair between London and Windermere. **Ham**mond and I would think nothing of putting ourselves in the **mail on** a Friday night, **and** coming down **to** spend Saturday **and** Sunday with you—if you are good.'

There came a sunny **morning** soon after Easter which **seemed mild** enough for June; and **when** Hammond **suggested that this was** the very day for Helvellyn, Maulevrier had not a word to say against the truth **of** that proposition. **The weather had been** exceptionally **warm for the** last week, and they had played tennis and **sat** in the garden **just** as if it had been actually summer. Patches of snow might still linger on the crests of the hills—but the approach to those bleak heights could hardly be glacial.

Mary clasped her hands delightedly.

'Dear old Maulevrier!' she exclaimed, 'you are always good to me. And now I shall be able to show you the Red Tarn, the highest pool of water in England,' she said, turning to Hammond. 'And you will see Windermere winding like a silvery serpent between the hills, and Grasmere shining like a jewel in the depth of the valley, and the sea glittering like a line of white light between the edges of earth and heaven, and the dark Scotch hills like couchant lions far away to the north.'

'That is to say these things are all supposed to be on view from the top of the mountain ; but as a peculiar and altogether exceptional state of the atmosphere is essential to their being seen, I need not tell you that they are rarely visible,' said Maulevrier. 'You are talking to old mountaineers, Molly. Hammond has done Cotapaxi and had his little clamber on the equatorial Andes, and I—well, child, I have done my Righi, and I have always found the boasted panorama enveloped in dense fog.'

'It won't be foggy to-day,' said Mary. 'Shall we do the whole thing on foot, or shall I order the ponies?'

Mr. Hammond inquired the distance up and down, and being told that it involved only a matter of eight miles, decided upon walking.

'I'll walk, and lead your pony,' he said to Mary, but Mary declared herself quite capable of going on foot, so the ponies were dispensed with as a possible encumbrance.

This was planned and discussed in the garden before breakfast. Fräulein was told that Mary was going for a long walk with her brother and Mr. Hammond; a walk which might last over the usual luncheon hour; so Fräulein was not to wait luncheon. Mary went to her grandmother's room to pay her duty visit. There were no letters for her to write that morning, so she was perfectly free.

The three pedestrians started an hour after breakfast, in light marching order. The two young men wore their Argyleshire shooting clothes— homespun knickerbockers and jackets, thick-ribbed hose knitted by Highland lasses in Inverness. They carried a couple of hunting flasks filled with claret, and a couple of sandwich boxes, and that was all. Mary wore her substantial tailor-gown of olive tweed, and a little toque to match, with a silver mounted grouse-claw for her only ornament.

It was a delicious morning, the air fresh and sweet, the sun comfortably warm, a little too warm, perhaps, presently, when they had trodden the narrow path by the Tongue Ghyll, and were beginning to wind slowly upwards over rough boulders and last year's bracken, tough and brown and tangled, towards that rugged wall of earth and stone tufted with rank grasses, which calls itself Dolly Waggon Pike. Here they all came to a stand-still, and wiped the dews of honest labour from their foreheads ; and here Maulevrier flung himself down upon a big boulder, with the soles of his stout shooting boots in running water, and took out his cigar case.

'How do you like it?' he asked his friend, when he had lighted his cigarette. 'I hope you are enjoying yourself.'

'I never was happier in my life,' answered Hammond.

He was standing on higher ground, with Mary at his elbow, pointing out and expatiating upon the details of the prospect. There were the lakes —Grasmere, a disk of shining blue; Rydal, a patch of silver; and Windermere winding amidst a labyrinth of wooded hills.

'Aren't you tired?' asked Maulevrier.

'Not a whit.'

'Oh, I forgot you had done Cotapaxi, or as much of Cotapaxi as living mortal ever has done. That makes a difference. I am going home.'

'Oh, Maulevrier!' exclaimed Mary, piteously.

'I am going home. You two can go to the top. You are both hardened mountaineers, and I am not in it with either of you. When I rashly consented to a pedestrian ascent of Helvellyn I had forgotten what the gentleman was like; and as to Dolly Waggon I had actually forgotten her existence. But now I see the lady—as steep as the side of a house, and as stony—no, naught but herself can be her parallel in stoniness. No, Molly, I will go no further.'

'But we shall go down on the other side,' urged Mary. 'It is a little steeper on the Cumberland side, but not nearly so far.'

'A little steeper! Can anything be steeper than Dolly Waggon? Yes, you are right. It *is* steeper on the Cumberland side. I remember coming down a sheer descent, like an exaggerated sugar-loaf; but I was on a pony, and it was the brute's look out. I will not go down the Cumberland side on my own legs. No, Molly, not even for you. But if you and Hammond want to go to the top, there is nothing to prevent you. He is a skilled mountaineer. I'll trust you with him.'

Mary blushed, and made no reply. Of all things in the world she least wanted to abandon the expedition. Yet to climb Helvellyn alone with her brother's friend would no doubt be a terrible violation of those laws of maidenly propriety which Fräulein was always expounding. If Mary were to do this thing, which she longed to do, she must hazard a lecture from her governess, and probably a biting reproof from her grandmother.

'Will you trust yourself with me, Lady Mary?' asked Hammond, looking at her with a gaze so earnest—so much more earnest than the occasion required—that her blushes deepened and her eyelids fell. 'I have done a good deal of climbing in my day, and I am not afraid of anything Helvellyn can do to me. I promise to take great care of you if you will come.'

How could she refuse? How could she for one moment pretend that she did not trust him, that her heart did not yearn to go with him. She would have climbed the shingly steep of Cotapaxi with him—or crossed the great Sahara with him—and feared nothing. Her trust in him was infinite—as infinite as her reverence and love.

'I am afraid Fräulein would make a fuss,' she faltered, after a pause.

'Hang Fräulein,' cried Maulevrier, puffing at his cigarette, and kicking about the stones in the clear running water. 'I'll square it with Fräulein. I'll give her a pint of fiz with her lunch, and make her see everything in a rosy hue. The good soul is fond of her Heidseck. You will be back by afternoon tea. Why should there be any fuss about the matter? Hammond wants to see the Red Tarn, and you are dying to show him the way. Go, and joy go with you both. Climbing a stony hill is a form of pleasure to which I have not yet risen. I shall stroll home at my leisure, and spend the afternoon on the billiard-room sofa reading Mudie's last contribution to the comforts of home.'

'What a Sybarite,' said Hammond. 'Come, Lady Mary, we mustn't loiter, if we are to be back at Fellside by five o'clock.'

Mary looked at her brother doubtfully, and he gave her a little nod which seemed to say, 'Go, by all means;' so she dug the end of her staff into Dolly's rugged breast, and mounted cheerily, stepping lightly from boulder to boulder.

The sun was not so warm as it had been ten minutes ago, when Maulevrier flung himself down to rest. The sky had clouded over a little, and a cooler wind was blowing across the breast of the hill. Fairfield yonder, that long smooth slope of verdure which a little while ago looked emerald green in the sunlight, now wore a soft and shadowy hue. All the world was greyer and dimmer in a moment, as it were, and Coniston Lake in its distant valley disappeared beneath a veil of mist, while the shimmering sea-line upon the verge of the horizon melted and vanished among the clouds that overhung it. The weather changes. very quickly in this part of the world. Sharp drops of rain came spitting at Hammond and Mary as they climbed the crest of the Pike, and stopped, somewhat breathless, to look back at Maulevrier. He was trudging blithely down the winding way, and seemed to have done wonders while they had been doing very little.

'How fast he is going,' said Mary.

'Easy is the descent of Avernus. He is going down-hill, and we are going upwards. That makes all the difference in life, you see,' answered Hammond.

Mary looked at him with divine compassion. She thought that for him the hill of life would be harder than Helvellyn. He was brave, honest, clever; but her grandmother had impressed upon her that modern civilisation hardly has room for a young man who wants to get on in the world, without either fortune or powerful connexions. He had better go to Australia and keep sheep, than attempt the impossible at home.

The rain was a passing shower, hardly worth speaking of, but the glory of the day was over. The sky was grey, and there were dark clouds creeping up from the sea-line. Silvery Windermere had taken a leaden hue; and now they turned their last fond look upon the Westmoreland valley, and set their faces steadily towards Cumberland, and the fine grassy plateau on the top of the hill.

All this was not done in a flash. It took them some time to scale Dolly's stubborn breast, and it took them another hour to reach Seat Sandal; and by the time they came to the iron gate in the fence, which at this point divides the two counties, the atmosphere had thickened ominously, and dark wreaths of fog were floating about and around them, whirled here and there by a boisterous wind which shrieked and roared at them with savage fury, as if it were the voice of some Titan monarch of the mountain protesting against this intrusion upon his domain.

'I'm afraid you won't see the Scottish hills,' shouted Mary, holding on her little cloth hat.

She was obliged to shout at the top of her voice, though she was close to Mr. Hammond's elbow, for that shrill screaming wind would have drowned the voice of a stentor.

'Never mind the view,' replied Hammond in the same fortissimo, 'but I really wish I hadn't brought you up here. If this fog should get any worse, it may be dangerous.'

'The fog is sure to get worse,' said Mary in

a brief lull of the hurly-burly, 'but there is no danger. I know every inch of the hill, and I am not a bit afraid. I can guide you, if you will trust me.'

'My bravest of girls,' he exclaimed, looking down at her. 'Trust you! Yes, I would trust my life to you—my soul—my honour—secure in your purity and good faith.'

Never had eyes of living man or woman looked down upon her with such tenderness, such fervent love. She looked up at him; looked with eyes which, at first bewildered, then grew bold, and lost themselves, as it were, in the dark grey depths of the eyes they met. The savage wind, hustling and howling, blew her nearer to him, as a reed is blown against a rock. Dark grey mists were rising round them like a sea; but had that ever thickening, ever darkening vapour been the sea itself, and death inevitable, Mary Haselden would have hardly cared. For in this moment the one precious gift for which her soul had long been yearning had been freely given to her. She knew all at once, that she was fondly loved by that one man whom she had chosen for her idol and her hero.

What matter that he was fortuneless, a nobody, with but the poorest chances of success in the world? What if he must needs, only to win the bare means of existence, go to Australia and keep sheep, or to the Red River valley and grow corn? What if he must labour, as the peasants laboured on the sides of this rude hill? Gladly would she go with him to a strange country, and keep his log cabin, and work for him, and share his toilsome life, rough or smooth. No loss of social rank could lessen her pride in him, her belief in him.

They were standing side by side a little way from the edge of the sheer descent, below which the Red Tarn showed black in a basin scooped out of the naked hill, like water held in the hollow of a giant's hand.

'Look,' cried Mary, pointing downward, 'you must see the Red Tarn, the highest water in England?'

But just at this moment there came a blast

which shook even Hammond's strong frame, and
with a cry of fear he snatched Mary in his arms
and carried her away from the edge of the hill.
He folded her in his arms and held her there,
thirty yards away from the precipice, safely
sheltered against his breast, while the wind raved
round them, blowing her hair from the broad,
white brow, and showing him that noble forehead in all its power and beauty; while the
darkness deepened round them so that they could
see hardly anything except each other's eyes.

'My love, my own dear love,' he murmured
fondly; 'I will trust you with my life. Will you
accept the trust? I am hardly worthy; for less
than a year ago I offered myself to your sister,
and I thought she was the only woman in this
wide world who could make me happy. And when
she refused me I was in despair, Mary; and I
left Fellside in the full belief that I had done
with life and happiness. And then I came back,
only to oblige Maulevrier, and determined to be
utterly miserable at Fellside. I was miserable for
the first two hours. Memories of dead and gone

joys and disappointed hopes were very bitter. And I tried honestly to keep up my feeling of wretchedness for the first few days. But it was no use, Molly. There was a genial spirit in the place, a laughing fairy who would not let me be sad; and I found myself becoming most unromantically happy, eating my breakfast with a hearty appetite, thinking my cup of afternoon tea nectar for love of the dear hand that gave it. And so, and so, till the new love, the purer and better love, grew and grew into a mighty tree, which was as an oak to an orchid, compared with that passion flower of earlier growth. Mary, will you trust your life to me, as I trust mine to you. I say to you almost in the words I spoke last year to Lesbia,' and here his tone grew grave almost to solemnity, 'trust me, and I will make your life free from the shadow of care—trust me, for I have a brave spirit and a strong arm to fight the battle of life—trust me, and I will win for you the position you have a right to occupy— trust me, and you shall never repent your trust.'

' She looked up at him with eyes which told of infinite faith, childlike, unquestioning faith.

'I will trust you in all things, and for ever,' she said. 'I am not afraid to face evil fortune. I do not care how poor you are—how hard our lives may be—if—if you are sure you love me.'

'Sure! There is not a beat of my heart or a thought of my mind that does not belong to you I am yours to the very depths of my soul. My innocent love, my clear-eyed, clear-souled angel! I have studied you and watched you and thought of you, and sounded the depths of your lovely nature, and the result is that you are for me earth's one woman. I will have no other, Mary, no other love, no other wife.'

'Lady Maulevrier will be dreadfully angry,' faltered Mary.

'Are you afraid of her anger?'

'No; I am afraid of nothing, for your sake.'

He lifted her hand to his lips and kissed it reverently, and there was a touch of chivalry in that reverential kiss. His eyes clouded with tears as he looked down into the trustful face. The fog had darkened to a denser blackness, and it was almost as if they were engulfed in sudden night.

'If we **are** never to find our way down the hill; if this were to be the last hour of **our lives**, Mary, would you be content?'

'Quite content,' she answered simply. 'I think I have **lived** long enough, if **you really love me** —if you are not making fun.'

'What, Molly, do you still **doubt**? Is it strange that I love you?'

'**Very** strange. I **am so** different from Lesbia.'

'**Yes**, very different, and the difference is your highest charm. **And now, love**, we had better go **down** whichever side **of** the hill is easiest, for this **fog** is rather appalling. I forgive the wind, because **it blew you** against my heart just now, **and that is where I want you** to dwell for ever.'

'**Don't** be frightened,' said Mary. 'I know every step of the way.'

So, leaning on her lover, and yet guiding him, slowly, **step by step, groping** their way through the darkness, Lady Mary led Mr. Hammond down the winding track along which the ponies and the guides travel so often in the summer season. And soon they began to descend out of that canopy of fog which enveloped the brow of Helvellyn, and to see the whole world smiling beneath them, a world of green pastures and sheep-folds, with a white homestead here and there amidst the fields, looking so human and so comfortable after that gloomy mountain top, round which the tempest howled so outrageously. Beyond those pastures stretched the dark waters of Thirlmere, looking like a broad river.

The descent was passing steep, but Hammond's strong arm and steady steps made Mary's progress very easy, while she had in no wise exaggerated her familiarity with the windings and twistings of the track. Yet as they had need to travel very slowly so long as the fog still surrounded them, the journey downward lasted a considerable time, and it was past five when they arrived at the little roadside inn at the foot of the hill.

Here Mr. Hammond insisted that Mary should rest at least long enough to take a cup of tea.

She was very white and tired. She had been profoundly agitated, and looked on the point of fainting, although she protested that she was quite ready to walk on.

'You are not going to walk another step,' said Hammond. 'While you are taking your tea I will get you a carriage.'

'Indeed, I had rather hurry on at once,' urged Mary. 'We are so late already.'

'You will get home all the sooner if you obey me. It is your duty to obey me now,' said Hammond, in a lowered voice.

She smiled at him, but it was a weak, wan little smile, for that descent in the wind and the fog had quite exhausted her. Mr. Hammond took her into a snug little parlour where there was a cheerful fire, and saw her comfortably seated in an arm-chair by the hearth, before he went to look after a carriage.

There was no such thing as a conveyance to be had, but the Windermere coach would pass in about half an hour, and for this they must wait. It would take them back to Grasmere sooner than they could get there on foot, in Mary's exhausted condition.

The tea-tray was brought in presently, and Hammond poured out the tea and waited upon Lady Mary. It was a reversal of the usual formula: but it was very pleasant to Mary to sit with her feet on the low brass fender, and to be waited upon by her lover. That fog on the brow of Helvellyn—that piercing wind—had chilled her to the bone, and there was unspeakable comfort in the glow and warmth of the fire, in the refreshment of a good cup of tea.

'Mary, you are my own property now, remember,' said Hammond, watching her tenderly as she sipped her tea.

She glanced up at him shyly, now and then, with eyes full of innocent wonder. It was so strange to her, as strange as sweet, to know that he loved her; such a marvellous thing that she had pledged herself to be his wife.

'You are my very own—mine to guard and cherish, mine to think and work for,' he went on, 'and you will have to trust me, sweet one ;

even if **the** beginning **of** things is not altogether free from trouble.'

'I am not afraid of trouble.'

'Bravely spoken. **First** and foremost then, you will have **to announce** your engagement to Lady Maulevrier. She will take it ill, no doubt; **will** do her utmost to persuade you to give me up. **Have you courage and resolution, do you** think, to stand against her arguments? Can you hold to your purpose bravely, and cry, no surrender?'

'**There shall be no surrender,**' answered Mary. 'I promise you that. No doubt grandmother **will** be very **angry.** But she **has never cared for me very much. It will not hurt her for me to make a bad match, as it** would have done in Lesbia's case. She has had no day-dreams—no grand ambition about me!'

'So much the better, my way-side flower. **When you have** said all that is sweet and dutiful **to her, and** have let her know at the same time that you mean to be my wife, come weal come woe I will see her, and will have my say. **I will not promise her a grand** career for my darling: but I will pledge myself that nothing of that kind which the world calls evil—no penury, or shabbiness of surroundings—shall ever touch Mary Haselden after she is Mary Hammond. I can promise at least so much as that.'

'It is more than enough,' said Mary. 'I have told you that I would gladly share poverty with you.'

'Sweet, it is good of you to say as much, but I would not take you at your word. You don't know what poverty is.'

'Do you think I am a coward, or self-indulgent? You are wrong, Jack. May I call you Jack, as Maulevrier does?'

'May you?'

The question evoked such a gush of tenderness that he was fain to kneel beside her chair and kiss the little hand holding the cup, before he considered he had answered properly.

'You are wrong, Jack. I do know what poverty means. I have studied the ways of the poor, tried to console them, and help them a little in their troubles; and I know there is no pain

that want of money can bring which I would
not share willingly with you. Do you suppose
my happiness is dependent on a fine house and
powdered footmen? I should like to go to the
Red River with you, and wear cotton gowns, and
tuck up my sleeves and clean our cottage.'

'Very pretty sport, dear, for a summer day;
but my Mary shall have a sweeter life, and shall
occasionally walk in silk attire.'

That tea-drinking by the fireside in the inn
parlour was the most delicious thing within John
Hammond's experience. Mary was a bewitching
compound of earnestness and simplicity, so
humble, so confiding, so perplexed and astounded
at her own bliss.

'Confess, now, in the summer, when you
were in love with Lesbia, you thought me a
horrid kind of girl,' she said, presently, when they
were standing side by side at the window, waiting
for the coach.

'Never, Mary. My crime is to have thought
very little about you in those days. I was so
dazzled by Lesbia's beauty, so charmed by her

accomplishments and girlish graces, that I forgot to take notice of anything else in the world. If I thought of you at all it was as another Maulevrier—a younger Maulevrier in petticoats, very gay, and good-humoured, and nice.'

'But when you saw me rushing about with the terriers—I must have seemed utterly horrid.'

'Why, dearest? There is nothing essentially horrible in terriers, or in a bright lively girl running races with them. You made a very pretty picture in the sunlight, with your hat hanging on your shoulder, and your curly brown hair and dancing hazel eyes. If I had not been deep in love with Lesbia's peerless complexion and Grecian features, I should have looked below the surface of that Gainsborough picture, and discovered what treasures of goodness, and courage, and truth and purity those frank brown eyes and that wide forehead betokened. I was sowing my wild oats last summer, Mary, and they brought me a crop of sorrow. But I am wiser now—wiser and happier.'

'But if you were to see Lesbia again, would not the old love revive?'

'The old love is dead, Mary. There is nothing left of it but a handful of ashes, which I scatter thus to the four winds,' with a wave of his hand towards the open casement. 'The new love absorbs and masters my being. If Lesbia were to re-appear at Fellside this evening, I could offer her my hand in all brotherly frankness, and ask her to accept me as a brother. Here comes the coach. We shall be at Fellside just in time for dinner.'

CHAPTER IV.

WISER THAN LESBIA.

Lady Mary and Mr. Hammond were back at
Fellside at a quarter before eight, by which
time the stars were shining on pine woods and
Fell. They managed to be in the drawing-room
when dinner was announced, after the hastiest
of toilets; yet her lover thought Mary had
never looked prettier than she looked that night,
in her limp white cashmere gown, and with
her brown hair brushed into a large loose knot
on the top of her head. There had been great
uneasiness about them at Fellside when evening
began to draw in, and the expected hour of
their return had gone by. Scouts had been sent
in quest of them, but in the wrong direction.

'I did not think you would be such idiots
as to come down the north side of the hill in

a tempest,' said Maulevrier; 'we could see the clouds racing over the crest of Seat Sandal, and knew it was blowing pretty hard up there, though it was calm enough down here.'

'Blowing pretty hard!' echoed Hammond, 'I don't think I was ever out in a worse gale; and yet I have been across the Bay of Biscay when the waves struck the side of the steamer like battering rams, and when the whole surface of the sea was white with seething foam.'

'It was a most imprudent thing to go up Helvellyn in such weather,' said Fräulein Müller, shaking her head gloomily as she ate her fish.

Mary felt that the Fräulein's manner boded ill. There was a storm brewing. A scolding was inevitable. Mary felt quite capable of doing battle with the Fräulein; but her feelings were altogether different when she thought of facing that stern old lady upstairs, and of the confession she had to make. It was not that her courage faltered. So far as resolution went she was as firm as a rock. But she felt that there was a terrible ordeal to be gone through; and it seemed a mockery to be sitting there and pretending to eat her dinner and take things lightly, with that ordeal before her.

'We did not go up the hill in bad weather, Miss Müller,' said Mr. Hammond. 'The sun was shining and the sky was blue when we started. We could not foresee darkness and storm at the top of the hill. That was the fortune of war.'

'I am very sorry Lady Mary had· not more good sense,' replied Fräulein with unabated gloom; but on this Maulevrier took up the cudgels.

'If there was any want of sense in the business, that's my look out, Fräulein,' he said, glaring angrily at the governess. 'It was I who advised Hammond and Lady Mary to climb the hill. And here they are, safe and sound after their journey. I see no reason why there should be any fuss about it.'

'People have different ways of looking at things,' replied Fräulein, plodding steadily on with her dinner.

Mary rose directly the dessert had been handed

round, and marched out of the room; like a warrior going to a battle in which the chances of defeat were strong. Fräulein Müller shuffled after her.

'Will you be kind enough to go to her ladyship's room at once, Lady Mary,' she said. 'She wants to speak to you.'

'And I want to speak to her,' said Mary.

She ran quickly upstairs and arrived in the morning room, a little out of breath. The room was lighted by one low moderator lamp, under a dark red velvet shade, and there was the glow of the wood fire, which gave a more cheerful light than the lamp. Lady Maulevrier was lying on her couch in a loose brocade tea-gown, with old Brussels collar and ruffles. She was as well dressed in her day of affliction and help-lessness as she had been in her day of strength; for she knew the value of surroundings, and that her stateliness and power were in some manner dependent on details of this kind. The one hand which she could use glittered with diamonds, as she waved it with a little imperious gesture towards the chair on which she desired Lady Mary to seat herself; and Mary sat down meekly, knowing that this chair represented the felon's dock.

'Mary,' began her grandmother, with freezing gravity, 'I have been surprised and shocked by your conduct to-day. Yes, surprised at such conduct *even* in you.'

'I do not think I have done anything very wrong, grandmother.'

'Not wrong! You have done nothing wrong? You have done something absolutely outrageous. You, my granddaughter, well born, well bred, reared under my roof, to go up Helvellyn and lose yourself in a fog alone with a young man. You could hardly have done worse if you were a Cockney tourist,' concluded her ladyship, with ineffable disgust.'

'I could not help the fog,' said Mary, quietly. The battle had to be fought, and she was not going to flinch. 'I had no intention of going up Helvellyn alone with Mr. Hammond. Maulevrier was to have gone with us; but when we got to

Dolly Waggon he was tired, and would not go any further. He told me to go on with Mr. Hammond.'

'*He* told you! Maulevrier!—a young man who has spent some of the best hours of his youth in the company of jockeys and trainers—who hasn't the faintest idea of the fitness of things. You allow Maulevrier to be your guide in a matter in which your own instinct should have guided you—your womanly instinct! But you have always been an unwomanly girl. You have put me to shame many a time by your hoydenish tricks; but I bore with you, believing that your madcap follies were at least harmless. To-day you have gone a step too far, and have been guilty of absolute impropriety, which I shall be very slow to pardon.'

'Perhaps you will be still more angry when you know all, grandmother,' said Mary.

Lady Maulevrier flashed her dark eyes at the girl with a look which would have almost killed a nervous subject; but Mary faced her steadfastly, very pale, but as resolute as her ladyship.

'When I know all! What more is there for me to know?'

'Only that while we were on the top of Helvellyn, in the fog and the wind, Mr. Hammond asked me to be his wife.'

'I am not surprised to hear it,' retorted her ladyship, with a harsh laugh. 'A girl who could act so boldly and flirtingly was a natural mark for an adventurer. Mr. Hammond no doubt has been told that you will have a little money by-and-by, and thinks he might do worse than marry you. And seeing how you have flung yourself at his head, he naturally concludes that you will not be too proud to accept your sister's leavings.'

'There is nothing gained by making cruel speeches, grandmother,' said Mary, firmly. 'I have promised to be John Hammond's wife, and there is nothing you nor anyone else can say which will make me alter my mind. I wish to act dutifully to you, if I can, and I hope you will be good to me and consent to this marriage. But if you will not consent, I shall marry him all the same. I shall be full of sorrow at having to disobey **you**; but **I** have promised, and **I** will keep **my promise.'**

'You will act in open rebellion against me— against **me** who has reared you, **and** educated you, and cared for you in all these years!'

'But you have never loved **me,'** answered Mary, sadly. 'Perhaps if you had given me some portion of that affection which you have lavished on **my sister I** might be willing to sacrifice this new deep **love for your** sake—to lay **down** my broken heart as **a** sacrifice on the altar of grati- tude. **But you** have **never loved me**; you have tolerated me, endured my presence as a disagreeable necessity **of your life,** because I am my father's daughter. You and Lesbia have been all the world to **each other, and I** have stood aloof, outside your charmed circle, almost **a** stranger to you. Can you **wonder,** grandmother, recalling this, that **I am** unwilling to surrender the love that has been given me to-day—the true, great heart of a brave and good man!'

·**Lady Maulevrier** looked at **her** for some

moments in scornful wonderment; looked at her with a slow, deliberate smile.

'Poor child!' she said; 'poor ignorant, inexperienced baby! For what a Will-o'-the-wisp are you ready to sacrifice my regard, and all the privileges of your position as my granddaughter! No doubt this Mr. Hammond has said all manner of fine things to you : but can you be weak enough to believe that he who half a year ago was sighing and dying at the feet of your sister can have one spark of genuine regard for you? The thing is not in nature; it is an obvious absurdity. But it is easy enough to understand that Mr. Hammond, without a penny in his pocket, and with his way to make in the world, would be very glad to secure Lady Mary Haselden and her five hundred a year, and to have Lord Maulevrier for his brother-in-law?'

'Have I really five hundred a year? Shall I have five hundred a year when I marry?' asked Mary, suddenly radiant.

'Yes; if you marry with your brother's consent.'

'I am so glad—for his sake. He could hardly

starve if I had five hundred a year. He need not be obliged to emigrate.'

'Has he been offering you the prospect of emigration as an additional inducement?'

'Oh, no, he does not say that he is very poor, but since you say he is penniless I thought we might be obliged to emigrate. But as I have five hundred a year ——'

'You will stay at home, and set up a lodging-house, I suppose,' sneered Lady Maulevrier.

'I will do anything my husband pleases. We can live in a humble way in some quiet part of London, while Mr. Hammond works at literature or politics. I am not afraid of poverty or trouble. I am willing to endure both for his sake.'

'You are a fool!' said her grandmother sternly. 'And I have nothing more to say to you. Go away, and send Maulevrier to me.'

Mary did not obey immediately. She went over to her grandmother's couch and knelt by her side, and kissed the poor maimed hand which lay on the velvet cushion.

'Dear grandmother,' she said gently. 'I am very sorry to rebel against you. But this is a question of life or death with me. I am not like Lesbia. I cannot barter love and truth for worldly advantage—for pride of race. Do not think me so weak or so vain as to be won by a few fine speeches from an adventurer. Mr. Hammond is no adventurer, he has made no fine speeches—but, I will tell you a secret, grandmother. I have liked and admired him from the first time he came here. I have looked up to him and reverenced him; and I must be a very foolish girl if my judgment is so poor that I can respect a worthless man.'

'You *are* a very foolish girl,' answered Lady Maulevrier, more kindly than she had spoken before, 'but you have been very good and dutiful to me since I have been ill, and I don't wish to forget that. I never said that Mr. Hammond was worthless; but I say that he is no fit husband for you. If you were as yielding and obedient as Lesbia it would be all the better for you; for then I should provide for your estab-

lishment in life in a becoming manner. But as you
are wilful, and bent upon taking your own way—
well—my dear, you must take the consequence ;
and when you are a struggling wife and mother,
old before your time, weighed down with the
weary burden of petty cares, do not say " My grandmother might have saved me from this martyrdom.' "

' I will run the risk, grandmother. I will be
answerable for my own fate.'

' So be it, Mary. And now send Maulevrier
to me.'

Mary went down to the billiard-room, where
she found her brother and her lover engaged in
a hundred game.

' Take my cue and beat him if you can, Molly,'
said Maulevrier, when he had heard Mary's mes-
sage. ' I'm fifteen ahead of him, for he has been
falling asleep over his shots. I suppose I am going
to get a lecture.'

' I don't think so,' said Mary.

' Well, my dearest, how did you fare in the
encounter ?' asked Hammond, directly Maulevrier
was gone

‘ Oh, it was dreadful ! I made the most rebellious speeches to poor grandmother, and then I remembered her affliction, and I asked her to forgive me, and just at the last she was ever so much kinder, and I think that she will let me marry you, now she knows I have made up my mind to be your wife—in spite of Fate.’

‘ My bravest and best.’

‘And do you know, Jack ’ — she blushed tremendously as she uttered this familiar name— ‘ I have made a discovery ?’

‘ Indeed ! ’

‘ I find that I am to have five hundred a year when I am married. It is not much. But I suppose it will help, won't it ? We can't exactly starve if we have five hundred a year. Let me see. It is more than a pound a day. A sovereign ought to go a long way in a small house ; and, of course, we shall begin in a very wee house, like De Quincey's cottage over there, only in London.’

‘ Yes, dear, there are plenty of such cottages in London. In Mayfair, for instance, or Belgravia.’

'Now, you are laughing at my rustic ignorance. But the five hundred pounds will be a help, won't it?'

'Yes, dear, a great help.'

'I'm so glad.'

She had chalked her cue while she was talking, but after taking her aim, she dropped her arm irresolutely.

'Do you know I'm afraid I *can't* play to-night,' she said. 'Helvellyn and the fog and the wind have quite spoilt my nerve. Shall we go to the drawing-room, and see if Fräulein has recovered from her gloomy fit?'

'I would rather stay here, where we are free to talk; but I'll do whatever you like best.'

Mary preferred the drawing-room. It was very sweet to be alone with her lover, but she was weighed down with confusion in his presence. The novelty, the wonderment of her position overpowered her. She yearned for the shelter of Fräulein Müller's wing, albeit the company of that most prosaic person was certain death to romance.

Miss Müller was in her accustomed seat by the fire, knitting her customary muffler. She had appropriated Lady Maulevrier's place, much to Mary's disgust. It irked the girl to see that stout, clumsy figure in the chair which had been filled by her grandmother's imperial form. The very room seemed vulgarised by the change.

Fräulein looked up with a surprised air when Mary and Hammond entered together, the girl smiling and happy. She had expected that Mary would have left her ladyship's room in tears, and would have retired to her own apartment to hide her swollen eyelids and humiliated aspect. But here she was, after the fiery ordeal of an interview with her offended grandmother, not in the least crestfallen.

'Are we not to have any tea to-night?' asked Mary, looking round the room.

'I think you are unconscious of the progress of time, Lady Mary,' answered Fräulein, stiffly. 'The tea has been brought in and taken out again.'

'Then it must be brought again, if Lady Mary

wauts some,' said Hammond, ringing the bell in the coolest manner.

Fräulein felt that things were coming to a pretty pass, if Maulevrier's humble friend was going to give orders in the house. Quiet and commonplace as the Hanoverian was, she had her ambition, and that was to grasp the household sceptre which Lady Maulevrier must needs in some wise resign, now that she was a prisoner to her rooms. But so far Fräulein had met with but small success in this endeavour. Her ladyship's authority still ruled the house. Her ladyship's keen intellect took cognisance even of trifles : and it was only in the·most insignificant details that Fräulein felt herself a power.

'Well, your ladyship, what's the row?' said Maulevrier, marching into his grandmother's room with a free and easy air.

He was prepared for a skirmish, and he meant to take the bull by the horns.

'I suppose you know what has happened to-day?' said her ladyship.

'Molly and Hammond's expedition, yes, of course. I went part of the way with them, but I was out of training, got pumped out after a couple of miles, and wasn't such a fool as to go to the top.'

'Do you know that Mr. Hammond made Mary an offer while they were on the hill, and that she accepted him ?'

'A queer place for a proposal, wasn't it ? The wind blowing great guns all the time. I should have chosen a more tranquil spot.'

'Maulevrier, cannot you be serious ? Do you forget that this business of to-day must affect your sister's welfare for the rest of her life ? '

'No, I do not. I will be as serious as a judge after he has put on the black cap,' said Maulevrier, seating himself near his grandmother's couch, and altering his tone altogether. 'Seriously I am very glad that Hammond has asked Mary to be his wife, and still more glad that she is tremendously in love with him. I told you some time ago not to put your spoke in that wheel. There could not be a happier or a better marriage for Mary.'

'You must have rather a poor opinion of your sister's attractions, personal or otherwise, if you consider a penniless young man—of no family—good enough for her.'

'I do not consider my sister a piece of merchandise to be sold to the highest bidder. Granted that Hammond is poor, and a nobody. He is an honourable man, highly gifted, brave as a lion, and he is my dearest friend. Can you wonder that I rejoice at my sister's having won him for her adoring lover?'

'Can he really care for her, after having loved Lesbia?'

'That was the desire of the eye, this is the love of the heart. I know that he loves Mary ever so much better than he loved Lesbia. I can assure your ladyship that I am not such a fool as I look. I am very fond of my sister Mary, and I have not been blind to her interests. I tell you, on my honour, that she ought to be very happy as John Hammond's wife.'

'I am obliged to believe what you say about is character,' said Lady Maulevrier. 'And I am willing to admit that the husband's character has a great deal to do with the wife's happiness, from a moral point of view; but still there are material questions to be considered. Has your friend *any* means of supporting a wife?'

'Yes, he *has* means; quite sufficient means for Mary's views, which are very simple.'

'You mean to say he would keep her in decent poverty? Cannot you be explicit, Maulevrier, and say what means the man has, whether any income or none? If you cannot tell me I must question Mr. Hammond himself.'

'Pray do not do that,' exclaimed her grandson urgently. 'Do not take all the flavour of romance out of Molly's love story, by going into pounds, shillings, and pence. She is very young. You would hardly wish her to marry immediately?'

'Not for the next year, at the very least.'

'Then why enter upon this sordid question of ways and means. Make Hammond and Mary happy by consenting to their engagement, and trust the rest to Providence, and to me. Take my word for it, Hammond is not a beggar, and

he is a man likely to make his mark in the
world. If a year hence his income is not enough
to allow of his marrying, I will double Mary's
allowance out of my own purse. Hammond's
friendship has steadied me, and saved me a good
deal more than five hundred a year.'

'I can quite believe that. I believe Mr.
Hammond is a worthy man, and that his
influence has been very good for you; but that
does not make him a good match for Mary.
However, you seem to have settled the business
among you, and I suppose I must submit. You
had better all drink tea with me to-morrow
afternoon; and I will receive your friend as
Mary's future husband.'

'That is the best and kindest of grandmothers.'

'But I should like to know more of his
antecedents and his relations.'

'His antecedents are altogether creditable.
He took honours at the University; he has been
liked and respected everywhere. He is an orphan,
and it is better not to talk to him of his
family. He is sensitive on that point, like most
men who stand alone in the world.'

'Well, I will hold my peace. You have taken this business into your hands, Maulevrier ; and you must be responsible for the result.'

Maulevrier left his grandmother soon after this, and went downstairs, whistling for very joyousness. Finding the billiard-room deserted he repaired to the drawing-room, where he found Mary playing scraps of melody to her lover at the shadowy end of the room, while Fräulein sat by the fire weaving her web as steadily as one of the Fatal Sisters, and with a brow prophetic of evil.

Maulevrier crept up to the piano, and came stealthily behind the lovers.

'Bless you, my children,' he said, hovering over them with outspread hands. ' I am the dove coming back to the ark. I am the bearer of happy tidings. Lady Maulevrier consents to your acquiring the legal right to make each other miserable for the rest of your lives.'

'God bless you, Maulevrier,' said Hammond, clasping him by the hand.

'Only as this sister of mine is hardly out

of the nursery you will have to wait for her
at least a year. So says the dowager, whose
word is like the law of the Medes and Persians,
and altereth not.'

'I would wait for her twice seven years, as
Jacob waited, and toil for her, as Jacob toiled,'
answered Hammond, ' but I should like to call
her my own to-morrow, if it were possible.'

Nothing could be happier or gayer than the
tea-drinking in Lady Maulevrier's room on the
following afternoon. Her ladyship having once
given way upon a point knew how to make her
concession gracefully. She extended her hand to
Mr. Hammond as frankly as if he had been her
own particular choice.

'I cannot refuse my granddaughter to her
brother's dearest friend,' she said, 'but I think
you are two most imprudent young people.'

'Providence takes care of imprudent lovers,
just as it does of the birds in their nests,'
answered Hammond, smiling.

'Just as much and no more, I fear. Pro-

vidence does not keep off the cat or the tax-
gatherer.'

'Birds must take care of their nests, and
husbands must work for their homes,' argued
Hammond. 'Heaven gives sweet air and sunlight,
and a beautiful world to live in.'

'I think,' said Lady Maulevrier, looking at
him critically, 'you are just the kind of person
who ought to emigrate. You have ideas that
would do for the Bush or the Yosemite Valley,
but which are too primitive for an over-crowded
country.'

'No, Lady Maulevrier, I am not going to steal
your granddaughter. When she is my wife she
shall live within call. I know she loves her native
land, and I don't think either of us would care
to put an ocean between us and rugged old
Helvellyn.'

'Of course having made idiots of yourselves up
there in the fog and the storm you are going to
worship the mountain for ever afterwards,' said
her ladyship laughing.

Never had she seemed gayer or brighter.

Perhaps in her heart of hearts she rejoiced at getting Mary engaged, even to so humble a suitor as fortuneless John Hammond. Ever since the visit of the so-called Rajah she had lived as Damocles lived, with the sword of destiny—the avenging sword—hanging over her by the finest hair. Every time she heard carriage wheels in the drive—every time the hall-door bell rang a little louder than usual, her heart seemed to stop beating and her whole being to hang suspended on a thread. If the thread were to snap, there must come darkness and death. The blow that had paralyzed one side of her body must needs, if repeated, bring total extinction. She who believed in no after life saw in her maimed and wasting arm the beginning of death. She who recognised only the life of the body felt that one half of her was already dead. But months had gone by, and Louis Asoph had made no sign. She began to hope that his boasted documents and witnesses were altogether mythical. And yet the engines of the law are slow to be put in motion. He might be working up his case, line upon line, with some hard-headed London lawyer; arranging and marshalling his facts; preparing his witnesses; waiting for affidavits from India; working slowly but surely, underground like the mole; and all at once, in an hour, his case might be before the law courts. His story and the story of Lord Maulevrier's infamy might be town talk again; as it had been forty years ago, when the true story of that crime had been happily unknown.

Yes, with the present fear of this Louis Asoph's revelations, of a new scandal, if not a calamity, Lady Maulevrier felt that it was a good thing to have her younger granddaughter's future in some measure secured. John Hammond had said of himself to Lesbia that he was not the kind of man to fail, and looking at him critically to-day Lady Maulevrier saw the stamp of power and dauntless courage in his countenance and bearing. It is the inner mind of a man which moulds the lines of his face and figure; and a man's character may be read in the way he walks and holds himself, the action of his hand, his smile, his frown, his general outlook, as clearly as in any phrenological development. John Hammond had a noble outlook : bold, without impudence or self-assertion ; self-possessed, without vanity. Yes, assuredly a man to wrestle with difficulty, and to conquer fate.

When that little tea-drinking was over and Maulevrier and his friend were going away to dress for dinner, Lady Maulevrier detained Mary for a minute or two by her couch. She took her by the hand with unaccustomed tenderness.

'My child, I congratulate you,' she said. 'Last night I thought you a fool, but I begin to think that you are wiser than Lesbia. You have won the heart of a noble young man.'

CHAPTER V.

'A YOUNG LAMB'S HEART AMONG THE FULL-GROWN
FLOCKS.'

FOR three most happy days Mary rejoiced in he
lover's society. Maulevrier was with them everywhere, by brookside and fell, on the lake, in the
gardens, in the billiard-room, playing propriety
with admirable patience. But this could not last
for ever. A man who has to win name and
fortune and a home for his young wife cannot
spend all his days in the primrose path. Fortunes
and reputations are not made in dawdling beside
a mountain stream, or watching the play of sunlight and shadow on a green hillside; unless,
indeed, one were a new Wordsworth, and even
then fortune and renown are not quickly made.

And again, Maulevrier, who had been a marvel
of good-nature and contentment for the last eight

weeks, was beginning to be tired of this lovely Lakeland. Just when Lakeland was daily developing into new beauty, Maulevrier began to feel an itching for London, where he had a comfortable nest in the Albany, and which was to his mind a metropolis expressly created as a centre or starting point for Newmarket, Epsom, Ascot, and Goodwood.

So there came a morning upon which Mary had to say good-bye to those two companions who had so blest and gladdened her life. It was a bright sunshiny morning, and all the world looked gay; which seemed very unkind of Nature, Mary thought. And yet, even in the sadness of this parting, she had much reason to be glad. As she stood with her lover in the library, in the three minutes of *tête-à-tête* stolen from the argus-eyed Fräulein, folded in his arms, looking up at his manly face, it seemed to her that the mere knowledge that she belonged to him and was beloved by him ought to sustain and console her even in long years of severance. Yes even if he were one of the knights of old, going to the Holy Land on a crusade full of peril and uncertainty. Even then a woman ought to be brave, having such a lover.

But her parting was to be only for a few months. Maulevrier promised to come back to Fellside for the August sports, and Hammond was to come with him. Three months—or a little more—and they were to meet again.

Yet in spite of these arguments for courage, Mary's face blanched and her eyes grew unutterably sad as she looked up at her lover.

'You will take care of yourself, Jack, for my sake, won't you, dear?' she murmured. 'If you should be ill while you are in London! If you should die ——'

'Life is very uncertain, love, but I don't feel like sickness or death just at present,' answered Hammond cheerily. 'Indeed, I feel that the present is full of sweetness, and the future full of hope. Don't suppose, dear, that I am not grieved at this good-bye : but before we are a year older I hope the time will have come when there will be no more farewells for you and me. I shall be a very exacting husband, Molly. I shall want to spend all the days and hours of my life with you ; to have not a fancy or a pursuit in which you cannot share, or with which you cannot sympathise. I hope you will not grow tired of me ! '

' Tired ! '

Then came silence, and a long farewell kiss, and then the voice of Maulevrier shouting in the hall, just in time to warn the lovers, before Miss Müller opened the door and exclaimed,

' Oh, Mr. Hammond, we have been looking for you *everywhere*. The luggage is all in the carriage, and Maulevrier says there is only just time to get to Windermere !'

In another minute or so the carriage was driving down the hill ; and Mary stood in the porch looking after the travellers.

' It seems as if it is my fate to stand here and see everybody drive away,' she said to herself.

And then she looked round at the lovely gardens, bright with spring flowers, the trees glorious with their young, fresh foliage, and the vast panorama of hill and dale, and felt that it was a wicked thing to murmur in the midst of such a world. And she remembered the great unhoped-for bliss that had come to her within the last four days, and the cloud upon her brow vanished, as she clasped her hands in childlike joyousness.

'God bless you, dear old Helvellyn,' she exclaimed, looking up at the sombre crest of the mountain. 'Perhaps if it had not been for you he would have never proposed.'

But she was obliged to dismiss this idea instantly; for to suppose John Hammond's avowal of his love an accident, the mere impulse of a weak moment, would be despair. Had he not told her how she had grown nearer and nearer to his heart, day by day, and hour by hour, until she had become part of his life? He had told her this—he, in whom she believed as in the very spirit of truth.

She wandered about the gardens for an hour after the carriage had started for Windermere, revisiting every spot where she and her lover had walked together within the last three days, living over again the rapture of those hours, repeating to herself his words, recalling his looks, with the fatuity of a first girlish love. And yet amidst the silliness inseparable from love's young dream, there was a depth of true womanly feeling, thoughtful, unselfish, forecasting a future which was not to travel always along the primrose path of dalliance —a future in which the roses were not always to be thornless.

John Hammond was going to London to work for a position in the world, to strive and labour among the seething mass of strugglers, all pressing onward for the same goal—independence, wealth, renown. Little as Mary knew of the world by experience, she had at least heard the wiseacres talk; and that which she had heard was calculated to depress rather than to inspire industrious youth. She had heard how the professions were all over-crowded: how a mighty army of young men were walking the hospitals, all intent on feeling the pulses and picking the pockets of the rising genera-tion: how at the Bar men were growing old and grey before they saw their first brief: how com-petitors were elbowing and hustling each other upon every road, thronging at every gate. And while masculine youth strove and wrestled for places in the race, aunts and sisters and cousins were pressing into the same arena, doing their best to crowd out the uncles and the brothers and the nephews.

'Poor Jack,' sighed Mary, 'at the worst we can go to the Red River country and grow corn.'

This was her favourite fancy, that she and her lover should find their first dwelling in the new world, live as humbly as the peasants lived round Grasmere, and patiently wait upon fortune. And yet that would not be happiness, unless Maulevrier were to come and stay with them every autumn. Nothing could reconcile Mary to being separated from Maulevrier for any lengthened period.

There were hours in which she was more hopeful, and defied the wiseacres. Clever young men had succeeded in the past—clever men whose hair was not yet grey had come to the front in the present. Granted that these were the exceptional men, the fine flower of humanity. Did she not know that John Hammond was as far above average youth as Helvellyn was above yonder mound in her grandmother's shrubbery?

Yes, he would succeed in literature, in politics, in whatever career he had chosen for himself. He was a man to do the thing he set himself to do, were it ever so difficult. To doubt his success would be to doubt his truth and his honesty: for he had sworn to her he would make her life bright and happy, and that evil days should never come to her: and he was not the man to promise that which he was not able to perform.

The house seemed terribly dull now that the two young men were gone. There was an oppressive silence in the rooms which had lately resounded with Maulevrier's frank, boyish laughter, and with his friend's deep, manly tones—a silence broken only by the click of Fräulein Müller's needles.

The Fräulein was not disposed to be sympathetic or agreeable about Lady Mary's engagement. Firstly, she had not been consulted about it. The thing had been done, she considered, in an underhand manner; and Lady Maulevrier, who had begun by strenuously opposing the match, had been talked over in a way that proved the latent weakness of that great lady's character. Secondly, Miss Müller, having herself for some reason missed such joys as are involved in being wooed and won, was disposed to look sourly upon all love-affairs, and to take a despondent view of all matrimonial engagements.

She did not say anything openly uncivil to Mary Haselden; but she let the damsel see that she pitied her and despised her infatuated condition; and this was so unpleasant that Mary was fain to fall back upon the society of ponies and terriers, and to take up her pilgrim's staff and go wandering over the hills, carrying her happy thoughts into solitary places, and sitting for hours in a heathery hollow, steeped in a sea of summer light, and trying to paint the mountain side and the rush of the waterfall. Her sketch-book was an excuse for hours of solitude, for the indulgence of an endless day-dream.

Sometimes she went among her humble friends in the Grasmere cottages, or in the villages of Great and Little Langdale; and she had now a new interest in these visits, for she had made up her mind that it was her solemn duty to learn housekeeping—not such housekeeping as might have been learnt at Fellside, supposing she had mustered the courage to ask the dignified upper-servants in that establishment to instruct her; but such domestic arts as are needed in the dwellings of the poor. The art of making a very little money go a great way; the art of giving grace, neatness, prettiness to the smallest rooms and the shabbiest furniture; the art of packing all the ugly appliances and baser necessities of daily life, the pots and kettles and brooms and pails, into the narrowest compass, and hiding them from the æsthetic eye. Mary thought that if she began by learning the homely devices of the villagers—the very A B C of cookery and housewifery—she might gradually enlarge upon this simple basis to suit an income of from five to seven hundred a year. The house-mothers from whom she sought information were puzzled at this sudden curiosity about domestic matters. They looked upon the thing as a freak of girlhood which drifted into eccentricity, from sheer idleness; yet they were not the less ready to teach Mary anything she desired to learn. They told her those secret arts by which coppers and brasses are made things of beauty, and meet adornment for an old oak mantelshelf. They allowed her to look on at the milking of the cow, and at the churning of the butter; and at bread making, and cake making, and pie and pudding making; and some pleasant hours were spent in the acquirement of this useful knowledge. Mary did not neglect the invalid during this new phase of her existence. Lady Maulevrier was a lover of routine, and she liked her granddaughter to go to her at the same hour every day. From eleven to twelve was the time for Mary's duty as amanuensis. Sometimes there were no letters to be written. Sometimes there were several; but her ladyship rarely allowed the task to go beyond the stroke of noon. At noon Mary was free, and free till five o'clock, when she was generally in attendance, ready to give Lady Maulevrier her afternoon tea, and sit and talk with her, and **tell** her **any scraps of local** news which she had **gathered in the day.**

There were days on which **her** ladyship preferred to take her tea **alone, and** Mary was left free to follow her own devices till dinner-time.

'I do not feel equal even **to your** society to-day, **my dear,'** her ladyship would **say**; 'go and enjoy **yourself** with **your** dogs and your tennis;' forgetting that there was **very** seldom anybody on the premises with whom Lady Mary could play tennis.'

But in these lonely days of Mary Haselden's life there **was** one crowning bliss which was almost enough to sweeten solitude, and take away the sting of separation; and that **was** the delight of expecting and receiving her lover's letters. Busily as Mr. Hammond must **needs** be **engaged** in fighting the battle of life, he was in no way wanting in his duty as a lover.   He **wrote** to Mary every other day; but though his letters were long, they told **her** hardly anything of himself or his occupation.   He wrote about pictures, books, music, such things as he knew must be interesting to her; but of his own struggles not a word.

'Poor fellow,' thought Mary. 'He is afraid to sadden me by telling me how hard the struggle is.'

Her own letters to her betrothed were simple outpourings of girlish love, breathing that too flattering-sweet idolatry which an innocent girl gives to her first lover. Mary wrote as if she herself were of the least possible value among created things.

With one of Mr. Hammond's earlier letters came the engagement ring; no half-hoop of brilliants or sapphires, rubies or emeralds, no gorgeous triple circlet of red, white, and green; but only a massive band of dead gold, on the inside of which was engraved this posy—'For ever.'

Mary thought it the loveliest ring she had ever seen in her life.

May was half over, and the last patch of snow had vanished from the crest of Helvellyn, from Eagle's Crag and Raven's Crag, and Coniston

Old Man. Spring—slow to come along these shadowy gorges—had come in real earnest now, spring that was almost summer ; and Lady Maulevrier's gardens were as lovely as dreamland. But it was an unpeopled paradise. Mary had the grounds all to herself, except at those stated times when the Fräulein, who was growing lazier and larger day by day in her leisurely and placid existence, took her morning and afternoon constitutional on the terrace in front of the drawing-room, or solemnly perambulated the shrubberies.

On fine days Mary lived in the garden, save when she was far afield learning the domestic arts from the cottagers. She read French and German, and worked conscientiously at her intellectual education, as well as at domestic economy. For she told herself that accomplishments and culture might be useful to her in her married life. She might be able to increase her husband's means by giving lessons abroad, or taking pupils at home. She was ready to do anything. She would teach the stupidest children, or scrub floors, or bake bread. There was no service she would deem degrading for his sake. She meant when she married to drop her courtesy title. She would not be Lady Mary Hammond, a poor sprig of nobility, but plain Mrs. Hammond, a working man's wife.

Lesbia's presentation was over, and had realised all Lady Kirkbank's expectations. The Society papers were unanimous in pronouncing Lord Maulevrier's sister the prettiest *débutante* of the season. They praised her classical features, the admirable poise of her head, her peerless complexion. They described her dress at the drawing-room ; they described her 'frocks' in the Park and at Sandown. They expatiated on the impression she had made at great assemblies. They hinted at even Royal admiration. All this, frivolous fribble though it might be, Lady Maulevrier read with delight, and she was still more gratified by Lesbia's own account of her successes. But as the season advanced Lesbia's letters to her grandmother grew briefer—mere hurried scrawls dashed off while the carriage was at the door, or while her maid was brushing her hair. Lady Maulevrier divined, with the keen instinct of love, that she counted for very little in Lesbia's life, now that the whirligig of society, the fret and fever of fashion, had begun.

One afternoon in May, at that hour when Hyde Park is fullest, and the carriages move slowly in triple rank along the Lady's Mile, and the mounted constables jog up and down with a business-like air which sets every one on the alert for the advent of the Princess of Wales, just at that hour when Lesbia sat in Lady Kirkbank's barouche, and distributed gracious bows and enthralling smiles to her numerous acquaintance, Mary rode slowly down the Fell, after a rambling ride on the safest and most 'venerable of mountain ponies. The pony was grey, and Mary was grey, for she wore a neat little homespun habit made by the local tailor, and a neat little felt hat with a ptarmigan's feather.

All was very quiet at Fellside as she went in at the stable gate. There was not an underling stirring in the large old stable yard which had remained almost unaltered for a century and a half; for Lady Maulevrier, whilst spending thousands on the new part of the house, had deemed the existing stables good enough for her stud. They were spacious old stables, built as solidly as a Norman castle, and with all the virtues and all the vices of their age.

Mary looked round her with a sigh. The stillness of the place was oppressive, and within doors she knew there would be the same stillness, made still more oppressive by the society of the Fräulein, who grew duller and duller every day, as it seemed to Mary.

She took her pony into the dusky old stable, where four other ponies began rattling their halters in the gloom, by way of greeting. A bundle of purple tares lay ready in a corner for Mary to feed her favourites; and for the next ten minutes or so she was happily employed going from stall to stall, and gratifying that inordinate appetite for green meat which seems natural to all horses.

Not a groom or stable boy appeared while she was in the stable; and she was just going

away, when her attention was caught by a flood
of sunshine streaming into an old disused harness-
room at the end of the stable—a room with one
small window facing the Fell.

Whence could that glow of western light come ?
assuredly not from the low-latticed window
which faced eastward, and was generally obscured
by a screen of cobwebs. The room was only
used as a storehouse for lumber, and it was nobody's
business to clean the window.

Mary looked in, curious to solve the riddle.
A door which she had often noticed, but never
seen opened, now stood wide open, and the old
quadrangular garden, which was James Steadman's
particular care, smiled at her in the golden evening
light. Seen thus, this little old Dutch garden
seemed to Mary the prettiest thing she had ever
looked upon. There were beds of tulips and
hyacinths, ranunculus, narcissus, tuberose, making
a blaze of colour against the old box borders, a
foot high. The crumbling old brick walls of the
out-buildings, and that dungeon-like wall which
formed the back of the new house, were clothed

with clematis and wistaria, woodbine and magnolia. All that loving labour could do had been done day by day for the last forty years to make this confined space a thing of beauty. Mary went out of the dark stable into the sunny garden, and looked round her, full of admiration for James Steadman's work.

'If ever Jack and I can afford to have a garden, I hope we shall be able to make it like this,' she thought. 'It is such a comfort to know that so small a garden can be pretty : for of course any garden we could afford must be small.'

Lady Mary had no idea that this quadrangle was spacious as compared with the narrow strip allotted to many a suburban villa calling itself 'an eligible residence.'

In the centre of the garden there was an old sundial, with a stone bench at the base, and, as she came upon an opening in the circular yew tree hedge which environed this sundial, and from which the flower beds radiated in a geometrical pattern, Lady Mary was surprised to see an old man—a very old man—sitting on this bench, and basking in the low light of the westering sun.

His figure was shrunken and bent, and he sat with his chin resting on the handle of a crutched stick, and his head leaning forward. His long white hair fell in thin straggling locks over the collar of his coat. He had an old-fashioned, mummyfied aspect, and Mary thought he must be very, very old.

Very, very old! In a flash there came back upon her the memory of John Hammond's curiosity about a hoary and withered old man whom he had met on the Fell in the early morning. She remembered how she had taken him to see old Sam Barlow, and how he had protested that Sam in no wise resembled the strange-looking old man of the Fell. And now here, close to the Fell, was a face and figure which in every detail resembled that ancient stranger whom Hammond had described so graphically.

It was very strange. Could this person be the same her lover had seen two months ago? And, if so, had he been living at Fellside all the time ; or was he only an occasional visitor of Steadman's ?

While she stood for a few moments meditating thus, the old man raised his head and looked up at her, with eyes that burned like red-hot coals under his shaggy white brows. The look scared her. There was something awful in it, like the gaze of an evil spirit, a soul in torment, and she began to move away, with sidelong steps, her eyes riveted on that uncanny countenance.

'Don't go,' said the man, with an authoritative air, rattling his bony fingers upon the bench. 'Sit down here by my side, and talk to me. Don't be frightened, child. You wouldn't, if you knew what they say of me indoors.' He made a motion of his head towards the windows of the old wing —"Harmless," they say, "quite harmless. Let him alone, he's harmless." A tiger with his claws cut and his teeth drawn—an old, grey-bearded tiger, ghastly and grim, but harmless—a cobra with the poison-bag plucked out of his jaw. The venom grows again, child—the snake's venom— but youth never comes back Old, and helpless, and harmless.'

Again Mary tried to move away, but those evil eyes held her as if she were a bird riveted by the gaze of a serpent.

'Why do you shrink away?' asked the old man, frowning at her. 'Sit down here, and let me talk to you. I am accustomed to be obeyed.'

Old and feeble and shrunken as he was, there was a power in his tone of command which Mary was unable to resist. She felt very sure that he was imbecile or mad. She knew that madmen are apt to imagine themselves great personages, and to take upon themselves, with a wonderful power of impersonation, the dignity and authority of their imaginary rank; and she supposed that it must be thus with this strange old man. She struggled against her sense of terror. After all there could be no real danger, in the broad daylight, within the precincts of her own home, within call of the household.

She seated herself on the bench by the unknown, willing to humour him a little; and he turned himself about slowly, as if every bone in his body were stiff with age, and looked at her with a deliberate scrutiny.

CHAPTER VI.

THE old man sat looking at Mary in silence for some moments ; not a great space of time, perhaps, as marked by the shadow on the dial behind them, but to Mary that gaze was unpleasantly prolonged. He looked at her as if he could read every pulsation in every fibre of her brain, and knew exactly what it meant.

'Who are you?' he asked, at last.

'My name is Mary Haselden.'

'Haselden,' he repeated, musingly, 'I have heard that name before.'

And then he resumed his former attitude, his chin resting on the handle of his crutch-stick, his eyes bent upon the gravel path, their unholy brightness hidden under the penthouse brows.

'Haselden,' he murmured, and repeated the

name over and over again, slowly, dreamily, with a troubled tone, like some one trying to work out a difficult problem. ' Haselden—when ? where ? '

And then with a profound sigh he muttered, ' Harmless, quite harmless. You may trust him anywhere. Memory a blank, a blank, a blank, my lord ! '

His head sank lower upon his breast, and again he sighed, the sigh of a spirit in torment, Mary thought. Her vivid imagination was already interested, her quick sympathies were awakened.

She looked at him wonderingly, compassion-ately. So old, so infirm, and with a mind astray ; and yet there were indications in his speech and manner that told of reason struggling against madness, like the light behind storm-clouds. He had tones that spoke of a keen sensitiveness to pain, not the lunatic's imbecile placidity. She observed him intently, trying to make out what manner of man he was.

He did not belong to the peasant class : of that she felt assured. The shrunken, tapering hand had never worked at peasant's work. The profile turned towards her was delicate to effeminacy. The man's clothes were shabby and old-fashioned, but they were a gentleman's garments, the cloth of a finer texture than she had ever seen worn by her brother. The coat, with its velvet collar, was of an old-world fashion. She remembered having seen just such a coat in an engraved portrait of Count d'Orsay, a print nearly fifty years old. No Dalesman born and bred ever wore such a coat; no tailor in the Dales could have made it.

The old man looked up after a long pause, during which Mary felt afraid to move. He looked at her again with inquiring eyes, as if her presence there had only just become known to him.

'Who are you?' he asked again.

'I told you my name just now. I am Mary Haselden.'

'Haselden— that is a name I knew—once. Mary? I think my mother's name was Mary. Yes, yes, I remember that. You have a sweet face, Mary—like my mother's. She had brown eyes, like yours, and auburn hair. You don't recollect her, perhaps?'

'Alas! poor maniac,' thought Mary, 'you have lost all count of time. Fifty years to you in the confusion of your distraught brain, are but as yesterday.'

'No, of course not, of course not,' he muttered; 'how should she recollect my mother, who died while I was a boy? Impossible. That must be half a century ago.'

'Good evening to you,' said Mary, rising with a great effort, so strong was her feeling of being spellbound by the uncanny old man, 'I must go indoors now.'

He stretched out his withered old hand, small, semi-transparent, with the blue veins showing darkly under the parchment-coloured skin, and grasped Mary's arm.

'Don't go,' he pleaded. 'I like your face, child; I like your voice—I like to have you here. What do mean by going indoors? Where do you live?'

'There,' said Mary, pointing to the dead wall

which faced them. 'In the new part of Fellside House. I suppose you are staying in the old part, with James Steadman.'

She had made up her mind that this crazy old man must be a relation of Steadman's, to whom he gave hospitality either with or without her ladyship's consent. All powerful as Lady Maulevrier had ever been in her own house, it was just possible that now, when she was a prisoner in her own rooms, certain small liberties might be taken, even by so faithful a servant as Steadman.

'Staying with James Steadman,' repeated the old man, in a meditative tone. 'Yes, I stay with Steadman. A good servant, a worthy person. It is only for a little while. I shall be leaving Westmoreland next week. And you live in that house, do you?' pointing to the dead wall. 'Whose house?'

'Lady Maulevrier's. I am Lady Maulevrier's granddaughter.'

'Lady Mau-lev-rier.' He repeated the name in syllables. 'A good name—an old title—as old as the conquest. A Norman race those Maulevriers. And you are Lady Maulevrier's granddaughter! You should be proud, The Maulevriers were always a proud race.'

'Then I am no true Maulevrier,' answered Mary, gaily.

She was beginning to feel more at her ease with the old man. He was evidently mad, as mad as a March hare; but his madness seemed only the harmless lunacy of extreme old age. He had flashes of reason, too. Mary began to feel a friendly interest in him. To youth in its flush of life and vigour there seems something so unspeakably sad and pitiable in feebleness and age—the brief weak remnant of life, the wreck of body and mind, sunning itself in the declining rays of a sun that is so soon to shine upon its grave.

'What, are you not proud?' asked the old man.

'Not at all. I have been taught to consider myself a very insignificant person; and I am going to marry a poor man. It would not become me to be proud.'

'But you ought not to do that,' said the old man. 'You ought not to marry a poor man. Poverty is a bad thing, my dear. You are a pretty girl, and ought to marry a man with a handsome fortune. Poor men have no pleasure in this world—they might just as well be dead. I am poor, as you see. You can tell by this threadbare coat'—he looked down at the sleeve from which the nap was worn in places—'I am as poor as a church mouse.'

'But you have kind friends, I dare say,' Mary said, soothingly. 'You are well taken care of, I am sure.'

'Yes, I am well taken care of—very well taken care of. How long is it, I wonder—how many weeks, or months, or years, since they have taken care of me? It seems a long, long time; but it is all like a dream—a long dream. Once I used to try and wake myself. I used to try and struggle out of that weary dream. But that was ages ago. I am satisfied now — I am quite content now—so long as the weather is warm, and I can sit out here in the sun.'

'It is growing chilly now,' said Mary, 'and I think you ought to go indoors. I know that I must go.'

'Yes, I must go in now—I am getting shivery,' answered the old man, meekly. 'But I want to see you again, Mary—I like your face—and I like your voice. It strikes a chord here,' touching his breast, 'which has long been silent. Let me see you again, child. When can I see you again?'

'Do you sit here every afternoon when it is fine?'

'Yes, every day—all day long sometimes when the sun is warm.'

'Then I will come here to see you.'

'You must keep it a secret, then,' said the old man, with a crafty look. 'If you don't they will shut me up in the house, perhaps. They don't like me to see people, for fear I should talk. I have heard Steadman say so. Yet what should I talk about, heaven help me? Steadman says my memory is quite gone, and that I am childish and harmless—childish and harmless. I have heard him say that. You'll come again, won't you, and you'll keep it a secret?'

Mary deliberated for a few minutes.

'I don't like secrets,' she said, 'there is generally something dishonourable in them. But this would be an innocent secret, wouldn't it? Well, I'll come to see you, somehow, poor old man; and if Steadman sees me here I will make everything right with him.'

'He mustn't see you here,' said the old man. 'If he does he will shut me up in my own rooms again, as he did once, years and years ago.'

'But you have not been here long, have you?' Mary asked, wonderingly.

'A hundred years, at least. That's what it seems to me sometimes. And yet there are times when it seems only a dream. Be sure you come again to-morrow.'

'Yes, I promise you to come; good-night.'

'Good-night.'

Mary went back to the stable. The door was still open, but how could she be sure that it would be open to-morrow? There was no other access that she knew of to the quadrangle, except through the old part of the house, and that was at all times inaccessible to her.

She found a key—a big old rusty key—in the inside of the door, so she shut and locked it, and put the key in her pocket. The door she supposed had been left open by accident; at any rate this key made her mistress of the situation. If any question should arise as to her conduct she could have an explanation with Steadman; but she had pledged her word to the poor mad old man, and she meant to keep her promise, if possible.

As she left the stable she saw Steadman riding towards the gate on his grey cob. She passed him as she went back to the house.

Next day, and the day after that, and for many days, Mary used her key, and went into the quadrangle at sundown to sit for half an hour or so with the strange old man, who seemed to take an intense pleasure in her company. The weather was growing warmer as May wore on towards June, and this evening hour, between six and seven, was deliciously bright and balmy. The seat by the sundial was screened on every side by the clipped yew hedge, dense and tall, surrounding the circular, gravelled space, in the centre of which stood the old granite dial, with its octagonal pedestal and moss-grown steps. There, as in a closely-shaded arbour, Lady Mary and her old friend were alone and unobserved. The yew-tree boundary was at least eight feet high, and Mary and her companion could hardly have been seen even from the upper windows of the low, old house.

Mary had fallen into the habit of going for her walk or her ride at five o'clock every day, when she was not in attendance on Lady Maulevrier, and after her walk or ride she slipped through the stable, and joined her ancient friend. Stables and courtyard were generally empty at this hour, the men only appearing at the sound of a big bell, which summoned them from their snuggery when they were wanted. Most of Lady Maulevrier's servants had arrived at that respectable stage of long service in which fidelity is counted as a substitute for hard work.

The old man was not particularly conversational, and was apt to repeat the same things over and over again, with a sublime unconsciousness of being prosy; but he liked to hear Mary talk, and he listened with seeming intelligence. He questioned her about the world outside his cloistered life—the wars and rumours of wars—and, although the names of the questions and the men of the day seemed utterly strange to him, and he had to have them repeated to him again and again, he seemed to take an intelligent interest in the stirring facts of the time, and listened intently when Mary gave him a synopsis of her last newspaper reading.

When the news was exhausted, Mary hit upon a more childish form of amusement, and that was to tell the story of any novel or poem she had been lately reading. This was so successful that in this manner Mary related the stories of most of Shakespeare's plays;

of Byron's Bride of Abydos, and Corsair ; of Keats's Lamia ; of Tennyson's Idylls ; and of a heterogenous collection of poetry and romance, in all of which stories the old man took a vivid interest.

'You are better to me than the sunshine,' he told Mary one day when she was leaving him. 'The world grows darker when you leave me.'

Once at this parting moment he took both her hands, and drew her nearer to him, peering into her face in the clear evening light.

'You are like my mother,' he said. 'Yes, you are very like her. And who else is it that you are like ? There is some one else, I know. Yes, some one else ! I remember ! It is a face in a picture—a picture at Maulevrier Castle.'

'What do you know of Maulevrier Castle ? ' asked Mary wonderingly.

Maulevrier was the family seat in Hereford-shire, which had not been occupied by the elder branch for the last forty years. Lady Maulevrier had let it during her son's minority to a younger branch of the family, a branch which had intermarried with the world of successful commerce, and was richer than the heads of the house. This occupation of Maulevrier Castle had continued to the present time, and was likely still to continue, Maulevrier having no desire to set up housekeeping in a feudal castle in the marches.

'How came you to know Maulevrier Castle?' repeated Mary.

'I was there once. There is a picture by Lely, a portrait of a Lady Maulevrier in Charles the Second's time. The face is yours, my love. I have heard of such hereditary faces. My mother was proud of resembling that portrait.'

'What did your mother know of Maulevrier Castle?'

The old man did not answer. He had lapsed into that dream-like condition into which he often sank, when his brain was not stimulated to attention and coherency by his interest in Mary's narrations.

Mary concluded that this man had once been a servant in the Maulevrier household, perhaps at the place in Herefordshire, and that all his old memories ran in one groove—the house of Maulevrier.

The freedom of her intercourse with him was undisturbed for about three weeks ; and at the end of that time she came face to face with James Steadman as she emerged from the circle of greenery.

'You here, Lady Mary ?' he exclaimed with an angry look.

'Yes, I have been sitting talking to that poor old man,' Mary answered, cheerily, concluding that Steadman's look of vexation arose from his being detected in the act of harbouring a contraband relation. 'He is a very interesting character. A relation of yours, I suppose ?'

'Yes, he is a relation,' replied Steadman. 'He is very old, and his mind has long been gone. Her ladyship is kind enough to allow me to give him a home in her house. He is quite harmless, and he is in nobody's way.'

'Of course not, poor soul. He is only a burden to himself. He talks as if his life had been very weary. Has he been long in that sad state?'

'Yes, a long time.'

Steadman's manner to Lady Mary was curt at the best of times. She had always stood somewhat in awe of him, as a person delegated with authority by her grandmother, a servant who was much more than a servant. But to-day his manner was more abrupt than usual.

'He spoke of Maulevrier Castle just now,' said Mary, determined not to be put down too easily. 'Was he once in service there?'

'He was. Pray how did you find your way into this garden, Lady Mary?'

'I came through the stable. As it is my grandmother's garden I suppose I did not take an unwarrantable liberty in coming,' said Mary, drawing herself up, and ready for battle.

'It is Lady Maulevrier's wish that this garden should be reserved for my use,' answered Steadman. 'Her ladyship knows that my uncle walks here of an afternoon, and that, owing to his age and infirmities, he can go nowhere else ; and if only on that account, it is well that the garden should be kept private. Lunatics are rather dangerous company, Lady Mary, and I advise you to give them a wide berth wherever you may meet them.'

'I am not afraid of your uncle,' said Mary, resolutely. 'You said yourself just now that he is quite harmless : and I am really interested in him, poor old creature. He likes me to sit with him a little of an afternoon and to talk to him; and if you have no objection I should like to do so, whenever the weather is fine enough for the poor old man to be out in the garden at this hour.'

'I have a very great objection, Lady Mary, and that objection is chiefly in your interest,' answered Steadman, firmly. 'No one who is not experienced in the ways of lunatics can imagine the danger of any association with them —their consummate craftiness, their capacity for crime. Every madman is harmless up to a certain point—mild, inoffensive, perhaps, up to the very moment in which he commits some appalling crime. And then people cry out upon the want of prudence, the want of common-sense which allowed such an act to be possible. No, Lady Mary, I understand the benevolence of your motive, but I cannot permit you to run such a risk.'

'I am convinced that the poor old creature is perfectly harmless,' said Mary, with suppressed indignation. 'I shall certainly ask Lady Maulevrier to speak to you on the subject. Perhaps her influence may induce you to be a little more considerate to your unhappy relation.'

'Lady Mary, I beg you not to say a word to Lady Maulevrier on this subject. You will do me the greatest injury if you speak of that man. I entreat you ——'

But Mary was gone. She passed Steadman with her head held high and her eyes sparkling with anger. All that was generous, compassionate, womanly in her nature was up in arms against her grandmother's steward. Of all other things,

Mary Haselden most detested cruelty; and she could see in Steadman's opposition to her wish nothing but the most cold-hearted cruelty to a poor dependent on his charity.

She went in at the stable door, shut and locked it, and put the key in her pocket as usual. But she had little hope that this mode of access would be left open to her. She knew enough of James Steadman's character, from hearsay rather than from experience, to feel sure that he would not easily give way. She was not surprised, therefore, on returning from her ride on the following afternoon, to find the disused harness-room half filled with trusses of straw, and the door of communication completely blocked. It would be impossible for her to remove that barricade without assistance; and then, how could she be sure that the door itself was not nailed up, or secured in some way ?

It was a delicious sunny afternoon, and she could picture the lonely old man sitting in his circle of greenery beside the dial, which for him had registered so many dreary and solitary hours, waiting for the little ray of social sunlight which her presence shed over his monotonous life. He had told her that she was like the sunshine to him—better than sunshine—and she had promised not to forsake him. She pictured him waiting, with his hands clasped upon his crutch-stick, his chin resting on his hands, his eyes poring on the ground, as she had seen him for the first time. And as the stable clock chimed the quarters he would begin slowly to think himself abandoned, forgotten; if, indeed, he took any count of the passage of time, of which she was not sure. His mind seemed to her to have sunk into a condition which was between dreaming and waking, a state in which the outside world seemed only half real—a phase of being in which there was neither past nor future, only the insufferable monotony of an everlasting *now*.

Pity is so near akin to love that Mary, in her deep compassion for this lonely, joyless, loveless existence, felt a regard which was almost affection for this strange old man, whose very name was unknown to her. True that there was much in his countenance and manner which was sinister and repellant. He was a being calculated to inspire fear rather than love; but the fact that he had courted her presence and looked to her for consolation had touched Mary's heart, and she had become reconciled to all that was forbidding and disagreeable in the lunatic's physiognomy. Was he not the victim of a visitation which entitled him to respect as well as to pity?

For some days Mary held her peace, remembering Steadman's vehement entreaty that she should not speak of this subject to her grandmother. She was silent, but the image of the old man haunted her at all times and seasons. She saw him even in her dreams—those happy dreams of the girl who loves and is beloved, and before whom the pathway of the future smiles like a vision of Paradise. She heard him calling to her with a piteous cry of distress, and on waking from this troubled dream she fancied that he must be dying, and that this

sound in her dreams was one of those ghostly warn-
ings which give notice of death. She was so unhappy about him, altogether so distressed at being
compelled to break her word, that she could not
prevent her thoughts from dwelling upon him, not
even after she had poured out all her trouble to
John Hammond in a long letter, in which her
garden adventures and her little skirmish with
Steadman were graphically described.

To her intense discomfiture Hammond replied
that he thoroughly approved of Steadman's conduct
in the matter. However agreeable Mary's society
might be to the lunatic, Mary's life was far too
precious to be put within the possibility of peril by
any such *tête-à-têtes*. If the person was the same
old man whom Hammond had seen on the Fell he
was a most sinister-looking creature, of whom any
evil act might be fairly anticipated. In a word Mr.
Hammond took Steadman's view of the matter, and
entreated his dearest Mary to be careful, and not to
allow her warm heart to place her in circumstances
of peril.

'This was most disappointing to Mary, who

expected her lover to agree with her upon every point; and if he had been at Fellside the difference of opinion might have given rise to their first quarrel. But as she had a few hours' leisure for reflection before the post went out, she had time to get over her anger, and to remember that promise of obedience given, half in jest, half in earnest, at the little inn beyond Dunmail Raise. So she wrote submissively enough, only with just a touch of reproach at Jack's want of compassion for a poor old man who had such strong claims upon everybody's pity.

The image of the poor old man was not to be banished from her thoughts, and on that very afternoon, when her letter was despatched, Mary went on a visit of exploration to the stables, to see if by any chance Mr. Steadman's plans for isolating his unhappy relative might be circumvented.

She went all over the stables — into loose boxes, harness and saddle rooms, sheds for wood, and sheds for roots, but she found no door opening into the quadrangle, save that door by which she had entered, and which was securely defended by a barricade of straw. that had been doubled by a fresh delivery of trusses since she first saw it. But while she was prowling about the sweet-scented stable, much disappointed at the result of her investigations, she stumbled against a ladder which led to an open trap-door. Mary mounted the ladder, and found herself amidst the dusty atmosphere of a large hayloft, half in shadow, half in the hot bright sunlight. A large shutter was open in the sloping roof, the roof that sloped towards the quadrangle, an open patch admitting light and air. Mary, light and active as a squirrel, sprang upon a truss of hay, and in another moment had swung herself into the opening of the shutter, and was standing with her feet on the wooden ledge at the bottom of the massive frame, and her figure supported against the slope of the thick thatched roof. Perched, or half suspended, thus, she was just high enough to look over the top of the yew-tree hedge into the circle round the sundial.

'Yes, there was the unhappy victim of fate,

and man's inhumanity to man.   There sat the shrunken figure, with drooping head, and melancholy attitude—the bent shoulders of feeble old age, the patriarchal locks so appealing to pity.   There he sat with eyes poring upon the ground, just as she had seen him the first time.   And while she had sat with him and talked with him he had seemed to awaken out of that dull despondency, gleams of pleasure had lighted up his wrinkled face — he had grown animated, a sentient living being instead of a corpse alive.   It was very hard that this little interval of life, these stray gleams of gladness should be denied to the poor old creature, at the behest of James Steadman.

Mary would have felt less angrily upon the subject had she believed in Steadman's supreme carefulness of her own safety; but in this she did not believe.   She looked upon the house-steward's prudence as a hypocritical pretence, an affectation of fidelity and wisdom, by which he contrived to gratify the evil tendencies of his own hard and cruel nature.   For some reason of his own, perhaps constrained thereto by necessity, he had given the

old man an asylum for his age and infirmity:
but while thus giving him shelter he considered
him a burden, and from mere perversity of mind
refused him all such consolations as were possible
to his afflicted state, mewed him up as a prisoner,
cut him off from the companionship of his fellow-
men.

Two years ago, before Mary emerged from her
Tomboyhood, she would have thought very little
of letting herself out of the loft window and
clambering down the side of the stable, which
was well furnished with those projections in the
way of gutters, drain-pipes, and century-old ivy,
which make such a descent easy. Two years ago
Mary's light figure would have swung itself down
among the ivy leaves, and she would have
gloried in the thought of circumventing James
Steadman so easily. But now Mary was a young
lady—a young lady engaged to be married, and
impressed with the responsibilities of her position,
deeply sensible of a new dignity, for the preservation of which she was in a manner answerable
to her lover.

VOL. II.   K

'What would *he* think of me if I went scrambling down the ivy?' she asked herself; 'and after he has approved of Steadman's heartless restrictions, it would be rank rebellion against him if I were to do it. Poor old man, "Thou art so near and yet so far," as Lesbia's song says.'

She blew a kiss on the tips of her fingers towards that sad solitary figure, and then dropped back into the dusty duskiness of the loft. But although her new ideas upon the subject of 'Anstand'—or good behaviour—prevented her getting the better of Steadman by foul means, she was all the more intent upon having her own way by fair means, now that the impression of the old man's sadness and solitude had been renewed by the sight of the drooping figure by the sundial.

She went back to the house, and walked straight to her grandmother's room. Lady Maulevrier's couch had been placed in front of the open window, from which she was watching the westward-sloping sun above the long line of hills, dark Helvellyn, rugged Nabb Scar, and verdant Fairfield, with its two giant arms stretched out to enfold and shelter the smiling valley.

'Heavens! child, what an object you are;' exclaimed her ladyship, as Mary drew near. 'Why, your gown is all over dust, and your hair is—why your hair is sprinkled with hay and clover. I thought you had learnt to be tidy, since your engagement. What have you been doing with yourself?'

'I have been up in the hayloft,' answered Mary, frankly; and, intent on one idea, she said impetuously, 'Dear grandmother, I want you to do me a favour—a very great favour. There is a poor old man, a relation of Steadman's, who lives with him, out of his mind, but quite harmless, and he is so sad and lonely, so dreadfully sad, and he likes me to sit with him in the garden, and tell him stories, and recite verses to him, poor soul, just as if he were a child, don't you know, and it is such a pleasure to me to be a little comfort to him in his lonely wretched life, and James Steadman says I mustn't go near him, because he may change at any moment into a dangerous lunatic, and do me some kind of harm, and I am not a bit afraid, and I'm sure he won't do anything of the kind, and, please grandmother, tell Steadman, that I am to be allowed to go and sit with his poor old prisoner half an hour every afternoon.'

Carried along the current of her own impetuous thoughts, Mary had talked very fast, and had not once looked at her grandmother while she was speaking. But now at the end of her speech her eyes sought Lady Maulevrier's face in gentle entreaty, and she recoiled involuntarily at the sight she saw there.

The classic features were distorted almost as they had been in the worst period of the paralytic seizure. Lady Maulevrier was ghastly pale, and her eyes glared with an awful fire as they gazed at Mary. Her whole frame was convulsed, and she, the cripple, whose right limbs lay numbed and motionless upon the couch, made a struggling motion as she raised herself a little with the left arm, as if, by very force of angry will, she would have lifted herself up erect before the girl who had offended her.

For a few moments her lips moved dumbly; and there was something unspeakably awful in those convulsed features, that livid countenance, and those voiceless syllables trembling upon the white dry lips.

At last speech came.

'Girl, you were created to torment me;' she exclaimed.

'Dear grandmother, what harm have I done?' faltered Mary.

'What harm? You are a spy. Your very existence is a torment and a danger. Would to God that you were married. Yes, married to a chimney-sweep, even — and out of my way.'

'If that is your only difficulty,' said Mary, haughtily, 'I dare say Mr. Hammond would be kind enough to marry me to-morrow, and take me out of your ladyship's way.'

Lady Maulevrier's head sank back upon her pillows, those velvet and satin pillows, rich with delicate point lace and crewel-work adornment, the labour of Mary and Fräulein, pillows which could not bring peace to the weary head, or deaden the tortures of memory. The pale face recovered its wonted calm, the heavy lids drooped over the weary eyes, and for a few moments there was silence in the room.

Then Lady Maulevrier raised her eyelids, and looked at her granddaughter imploringly, pathetically.

'Forgive me, Mary,' she said. 'I don't know what I was saying just now; but whatever it was, forgive and forget it. I am a wretched old woman, heart sick, heart sore, worn out by pain and weariness. There are times when I am beside myself; moments when I am not much saner than Steadman's lunatic uncle. This is one of my worst days, and you came bouncing in upon me, and tortured my nerves by your breathless torrent of words. Pray forgive me, if I said anything rude.'

'If,' thought Mary: but she tried to be charitable, and to believe that Lady Maulevrier's attack upon her was a new phase of hysteria, so she murmured meekly, 'There is nothing for me to forgive, grandmother, and I am very sorry I disturbed you.'

She was going to leave the room, thinking that her absence would be a relief to the invalid, when Lady Maulevrier called her back.

'You were asking me something—something about that old man of Steadman's,' she said with a weary air, half indifference, half the lassitude natural to an invalid who sinks under the burden of monotonous days. 'What was it all about? I forget.'

Mary repeated her request, but this time in measured tones.

'My dear, I am sure that Steadman was only properly prudent,' answered Lady Maulevrier, 'and that it would never do for me to interfere in this matter. It stands to reason that he must know his old kinsman's temperament much better than you can, after your half-hour interviews with him in the garden. Pray how long have these garden scenes been going on, by-the-by ?' asked her ladyship, with a searching look at Mary's downcast face.

The girl had not altogether recovered from the rude shook of her grandmother's late attack.

'About three weeks,' faltered Mary. 'But it is more than a week now since I was in the garden. It was quite by accident that I first went there. Perhaps I ought to explain.'

And Mary, not being gainsayed, went on to describe that first afternoon when she had seen the old man brooding in the sun. She drew quite a pathetic picture of his joyless solitude, whilst all nature around and about him was looking so glad in the spring sunshine. There was a long silence, a silence of some minutes, when she had done; and Lady Maulevrier lay with lowered eyelids, deep in thought. Mary began to hope that she had touched her grandmother's heart, and that her request would be granted: but she was soon undeceived.

'I am sorry to be obliged to refuse you a favour, Mary, but I must stand by Steadman,' said her ladyship. 'When I gave Steadman permission to shelter his aged kinsman in my house, I made it a condition that the old man should be kept in the strictest care by himself and his wife, and that nobody in this establishment should be troubled by him. This condition has been so scrupulously adhered to that the old man's existence is known to no one in this house except you and me; and you have discovered the fact only by accident. I must beg you to keep this secret to yourself. Steadman has particular reasons for wishing to conceal the fact of his uncle's residence here. The old man is not actually a lunatic. If he were we should be violating the law by keeping him here. He is only imbecile from extreme old age; the body has outlived the mind, that is all. But should any officious functionary come down upon Fellside, this imbecility might be called madness, and the poor old creature whom you regard so compassionately, and whose case you think so pitiable here, would be carried off to a pauper lunatic asylum, which I can assure you would be a much worse imprisonment than Fellside Manor.'

'Yes, indeed, grandmother,' exclaimed Mary, whose vivid imagination conjured up a vision of padded cells, strait-waistcoats, murderously-inclined keepers, chains, handcuffs, and bread and water diet; 'now I understand why the poor old soul has been kept so close—why nobody knows of his existence. I beg Steadman's pardon with all my heart. He is a much better fellow than I thought him.'

'Steadman is a thoroughly good fellow, and as true as steel,' said her ladyship. 'No one can know that so well as the mistress he has served faithfully for nearly half a century. I hope, Mary, you have not been chattering to Fräulein or any one else about your discovery.'

'No, grandmother, I have not said a word to a mortal, but ——'

'Oh, there is a "but," is there? I understand. You have not been so reticent in your letters to Mr. Hammond.'

'I tell him all that happens to me. There is very little to write about at Fellside; yet I contrive to send him volumes. I often wonder what poor girls did in the days of Miss Austen's novels, when letters cost a shilling or eighteen pence for postage, and had to be paid for by the recipient. It must have been such a terrible check upon affection.'

'And upon twaddle,' said Lady Maulevrier. 'Well, you told Mr. Hammond about Steadman's old uncle. What did he say?'

'He thoroughly approved Steadman's conduct in forbidding me to go and see him,' answered Mary. 'I couldn't help thinking it rather unkind of him; but, of course, I feel that he must be right,' concluded Mary, as much as to say that her lover was necessarily infallible.

'I always thought Mr. Hammond a sensible young man, and I am glad to find that his conduct does not belie my good opinion,' said Lady Maulevrier. 'And now, my dear, you had better go and make yourself decent before dinner. I am very weary this afternoon, and even our little talk has exhausted me.'

'Yes, dear grandmother, I am going this instant.

But let me ask one question: What is the poor old man's name?'

'His name!' said her ladyship, looking at Mary with a puzzled air, like a person whose thoughts are far away. 'His name—oh, Steadman, I suppose, like his nephew's; but if I ever heard the name I have forgotten it, and I don't know whether the kinship is on the father's or the mother's side. Steadman asked my permission to give shelter to a helpless old relative, and I gave it. That is really all I remember.'

'Only one other question,' pleaded Mary, who was brimful of curiosity upon this particular subject. 'Has he been at Fellside very long?'

'Oh, I really don't know; a year, or two, or three, perhaps. Life in this house is all of a piece. I hardly keep count of time.'

'There is one thing that puzzles me very much,' said Mary, still lingering near her grandmother's couch, the balmy evening air caressing her as she leaned against the embrasure of the wide Tudor window, the sun drawing nearer to the edge of the hills, an orb of yellow flame, soon to change to a gigantic disk of lurid fire. 'I thought from the old man's talk that he, too, must be an old servant in our family. He talked of Maulevrier Castle, and said that I reminded him of a picture by Lely, a portrait of a Lady Maulevrier.'

'It is quite possible that he may have been in service there, though I do not remember to have heard anything about it,' answered her ladyship, carelessly. 'The Steadmans come from that part of the country, and theirs is a hereditary service. Good-night, Mary, I am utterly weary. Look at that glorious light yonder, that mighty world of fire and flame, without which our little world would be dark and dreary. I often think of that speech of Macbeth's, "I 'gin to be aweary of the sun." There comes a time, Mary, when even the sun is a burden.'

'Only for such a man as Macbeth,' said Mary, 'a man steeped in crime. Who can wonder that he wanted to hide himself from the sun? But, dear grandmother, there ought to be plenty of happiness left for you, even if your recovery is slow to come. You are so clever, you have such resources in your own mind and memory, and you have your grandchildren, who love you dearly,' added Mary, tenderly.

Her nature was so full of pity that an entirely new affection had grown up in her mind for Lady Maulevrier since that terrible evening of the paralytic stroke.

'Yes, and whose love, as exemplified by Lesbia, is shown in a hurried scrap of a letter scrawled once a week—a bone thrown to a hungry dog,' said her ladyship, bitterly.

'Lesbia is so lovely, and she is so surrounded by flatterers and admirers,' murmured Mary, excusingly.

'Oh, my dear, if she had a heart she would not forget me, even in the midst of her flatterers. Good-night again, Mary. Don't try to console me. For some natures consolations and soothing suggestions are like flowers thrown upon a granite tomb. They do just as much and just as little good to the heart that lies under the stone. Goodnight.'

Mary stooped to kiss her grandmother's fore-

head, and found it cold as marble. She murmured
a loving good-night, and left the mistress of Fellside
in her loneliness.

A footman would come in and light the lamps,
and draw the velvet curtains, presently, and shut
out the later glories of sunset. And then the
butler himself would come and arrange the little
dinner table by her ladyship's couch, and would
himself preside over the invalid's simple dinner,
which would be served exquisitely, with all that
is daintiest and most costly in Salviati glass and
antique silver. Yet better the dinner of herbs,
and love and peace withal, than the choicest fare
or the most perfect service.

Before the coming of the servants and the
lamps there was a pause of silence and loneliness,
an interval during which Lady Maulevrier lay
gazing at the declining orb, the lower rim of
which now rested on the edge of the hill. It
seemed to grow larger and more dazzling as she
looked at it.

Suddenly she clasped her left hand across her
eyes, and said aloud—

‘ Oh, what a hateful life! Almost half a century of lies and hypocricies and prevarications and meannesses! For what? For the glory of an empty name ; and for a fortune that may slip from my dead hand to become the prey of rogues and adventurers. Who can forecast the future ? ’

CHAPTER VII.

LADY KIRKBANK'S house in Arlington Street was known to half fashionable London as one of the pleasantest houses in town ; and it was known by repute only, to the other half of fashionable London, as a house whose threshold was not to be crossed by persons with any regard for their own dignity and reputation. It was not that Lady Kirkbank had ever actually forfeited her right to be considered an honest woman and a faithful wife. People who talked of the lady and her set with a contemptuous shrug of the shoulders and a dubious elevation of the eyebrows were ready, when hard pushed in argument, to admit that they knew of no actual harm in Lady Kirkbank, no overt bad behaviour. 'But—well,' said the punctilious half of society, the Pejinks and Pernickitys, the Picksomes and Unco-Goods, 'Lady Kirkbank is—Lady Kirkbank; and I would not allow my girls to visit her, don't you know.' 'Lady Kirkbank is received, certainly,' said a severe dowager. 'She goes to very good houses. She gets tickets for the Royal enclosure. She is always at private views, and privileged shows of all kinds; and she contrives to squeeze herself in at a State ball or a concert about once in two years; but any one who can consider Lady Kirkbank good style must have a very curious idea of what a lady ought to be.' 'Lady Kirkbank is a warm-hearted, nice creature,' said a diplomatist of high rank, and one of her particular friends, 'but her manners are decidedly—continental!'

About Sir George, society, adverse or friendly, was without strong opinions. His friends, the men who shot over his Scotch moor, and filled the spare rooms in his villa at Cannes, and loaded his drag for Sandown or Epsom, and sponged upon him all the year round, talked of him as 'an inoffensive old party,' 'a cheery soul,' 'a genial old boy,' and in like terms of approval.

That half of society which did not visit in Arlington Street, in whose nostrils the semi-aristocratic, semi-artistic, altogether Bohemian little dinners, the suppers after the play, the small hours devoted to Nap or Poker, had an odour as of sulphur, the reek of Tophet—even this half of the great world was fain to admit that Sir George was harmless. He had never had an idea beyond the realms of sport; he had never had a will of his own outside his stable. To shoot pigeons at Hurlingham or Monaco, to keep half a dozen leather-platers, and attend every race from the Craven to the Leger, to hunt four days a week, when he was allowed to spend a winter in England, and to saunter and sleep away all the hours which could not be given to sport, comprised Sir George's idea of existence. He had never troubled himself to consider whether there might not possibly be a better way of getting rid of one's life. He was as God had made him, and was perfectly satisfied with himself and the universe; save at such times as when a favourite horse went lame, or his banker wrote to tell him that his account was overdrawn.

Sir George had no children; he had never had a serious care in his life. He never thought, he never read. Lady Kirkbank declared that she had never seen him with a book in his hands since their marriage.

'I don't believe he would know at which end to begin,' she said.

What was the specific charge which the very particular people brought against Lady Kirkbank? Such charges rarely *are* specific. The idea that the lady belonged to the fast and furious section of society, the Bohemia of the upper ten, was an idea in the air. Everybody knew it. No one could quite adequately explain it.

From thirty to fifty Lady Kirkbank had been known as a flirty matron. Wherever she went, a train of men went with her; men young and middle-aged and elderly; handsome youths from the public offices; War, Admiralty, Foreign Office, Somerset House young men; attractive men of mature years, with grey moustachios, military, diplomatic, horsey, what you will, but always agreeable. At home, abroad, Lady Kirkbank was never without her court; but the court was entirely masculine. In those days the fair Georgie did not scruple to say that she hated women, and that girls were her particular abomination. But as the years rolled on Lady Kirkbank began to find it very difficult to muster her little court, to keep her train in attendance upon her. 'The birds were wild,' Sir George said. Her young adorers found their official duties more oppressive than hitherto; her elderly swains had threatenings of gout or rheumatism which prevented their flocking round her as of old at race meeting or polo match. They were loyal enough in keeping their engagements at the dinner table, for Lady Kirkbank's cook was one of the best in London; and the invited guests were rarely missing at the little suppers after opera or play; but Georgie's box was no longer crowded with men who dropped in between the acts to see what she thought of the singer or the piece, and her swains were no longer contented to sit behind her chair all the evening, seeing an empty corner of the stage across Georgie's ivory shoulder, and hearing the voices of invisible actors in the brief pauses of Georgie's subdued babble.

At fifty-five, Georgina Kirkbank told herself sadly enough that her day, as a bright particular star, all-sufficient in her own radiance, was gone. She could not live without her masculine circle, men who could bring her all the news, the gossip of the clubs; where everything seemed to become known as quickly as if each club had its own Asmodeus, unroofing all the housetops of the West End for inspection every night. She could not live without her courtiers; and to keep them about her she knew that she must make her house pleasant. It was not enough to give good dinners, elegant little suppers washed down by choicest wines; she must also provide fair faces to smile upon the feast, and bright eyes to sparkle in the subdued light of low shaded lamps, and many candles twinkling under coloured shades.

'I am an old woman now,' Lady Kirkbank said to herself with a sigh,' and my own attractions won't keep my friends about me. *C'est trop connu ça.*'

And now the house in Arlington Street in which feminine guests had been as one in ten, opened its doors to the young and the fair. Pretty widows, lively girls, young wives who were not too absurdly devoted to their husbands, actresses of high standing and good looks, these began to be welcomed effusively in Arlington Street. Lady Kirkbank began to hunt for beauties to adorn her rooms, as she had hitherto hunted lions to roar at her parties. She prided herself on being the first to discover this or that new beauty. That lovely girl from Scotland with the large eyes—that sweet young creature from Ireland with the long eyelashes. She was always inventing new divinities. But even this change of plan, this more feminine line of politics failed to reconcile the strict and the stern, the Queen Charlotte-ish elderly ladies, and the impeccable matrons, to Lady Kirkbank and her set. The girls who were launched by Lady Kirkbank never took high rank in society. When they made good marriages it was generally to be observed that they dropped Lady Kirkbank soon afterwards. It was not their fault, these ingrates pleaded piteously; but Edward, or Henry, or Theodore, as the case might be, had a most cruel prejudice against dear Lady Kirkbank, and the young wives were obliged to obey.

Others there were, however, the loyal few, who having won the prize matrimonial in Lady Kirkbank's happy hunting grounds, remained true to their friend ever afterwards, and defended her character against every onslaught.

When Lady Maulevrier told her grandson that she had entrusted Lady Kirkbank with the duty of introducing Lesbia to society, Maulevrier shrugged his shoulders and held his peace. He knew no actual harm in the matter. Lady Kirkbank's was rather a fast set; and had he been allowed to choose it was not to Lady Kirkbank that he would have delegated his grandmother's duty. In Maulevrier's own phrase it was 'not good enough' for Lesbia. But it was not in his power to interfere. He was not told of the plan until everything had been set-tled. The thing was accomplished; and against accomplished facts Maulevrier was the last to protest.

His friend John Hammond had not been silent. He knew nothing of Lady Kirkbank personally; but he knew the position which she held in London society, and he urged his friend strongly to enlighten Lady Maulevrier as to the kind of circle into which she was about to entrust her young granddaughter, a girl brought up in the Arcadia of England.

'Not for worlds would I undertake such a task,' said Maulevrier. 'Her ladyship never had any opinion of my wisdom, and this Lady Kirkbank is a friend of her own youth. She would cut up rough if I were to say a word against an old friend. Besides what's the odds, if you come to think of it? all society is fast now-a-days, or at any rate all society worth living in. And then again, Lesbia is just one of those cool-headed girls who would keep herself head uppermost in a maelstrom. She knows on which side her bread is buttered. Look how easily she chucked you up because she did not think you good enough. She'll make use of this Lady Kirkbank, who is a good soul, I am told, and will make the best match of the season.'

And now the season had begun, and Lady Lesbia Haselden was circulating with other aristocratic atoms in the social vortex, with her head apparently uppermost.

'Old Lady K— has nobbled a real beauty, this time,' said one of the Arlington Street set to his friend as they lolled on the railings in the park, 'a long way above any of those plainheaded ones she tried to palm off upon us last year: the South American girl with the big eyes and a complexion like a toad, the Forfarshire girl with freckles and unsophisticated carrots. "Those lovely Spanish eyes," said Lady K—, "that Titianesque auburn hair!" But it didn't answer. Both the girls were plain, and they have gone back to their native obscurity spinsters still. But this is a real thorough-bred one—blood, form, pace, all there.'

'Who is she?' drawled his friend.

'Lord Maulevrier's sister, Lady Lesbia Haselden. Has money, too, I believe; rich grand-mother; old lady buried alive in Westmoreland; horrid old miser.'

'I shouldn't mind marrying a miser's grand-daughter,' said the other. 'So nice to know that some wretched old idiot has scraped and hoarded through a lifetime of deprivation and self-denial, in order that one may spend his money when he is under the sod.'

Lady Lesbia was accepted everywhere, or almost everywhere, as the beauty of the season. There were six or seven other girls who aspired to the same proud position, who were asserted by their own particular friends to have won it; just as there are generally four or five horses which claim to be first favourites; but the betting was all in favour of Lady Lesbia.

Lady Kirkbank told her that she was turning everyone's head, and Lesbia was quite willing to believe her. But was Lesbia's own head quite steady in this whirlpool? That was a question which she did not take the trouble to ask her-self.

Her heart was tranquil enough, cold as marble. No shield and safeguard so secure against the fire of new love as an old love hardly cold. Lesbia told herself that her heart was a sepulchre, an urn which held a handful of ashes, the ashes of her passion for John Hammond. It was a fire quite burned out, she thought; but that extinguished flame had left death-like coldness.

This was Lesbia's own diagnosis of her case: but the real truth was that among the herd of men she had met, almost all of them ready to fall down and worship her, there was not one who had caught her fancy. Her nature was shallow enough to be passing fickle; the passion which she had taken for love was little more than a girl's fancy; but the man who had power to awaken that fancy as John Hammond had done had not yet appeared in Lady Kirkbank's circle.

'What a cold-hearted creature you must be,' said Georgie. 'You don't seem to admire any of my favourite men.'

'They are very nice,' Lesbia answered languidly; 'but they are all alike. They say the same things—wear the same clothes—sit in the same attitude. One would think they were all drilled in a body every morning before they go out. Mr. Nightshade, the actor, who came to supper the other night, is the only man I have seen who has a spark of originality.'

'You are right,' answered Lady Kirkbank, 'there is an appalling sameness in men: only it is odd you should find it out so soon. I never discovered it till I was an old woman. How I envy Cleopatra her Cæsar and her Antony. No mistaking one of those for the other. Mary Stuart too, what marked varieties of character she had an opportunity of studying in Rizzio and Chastelard, Darnley and Bothwell. Ah, child, that is what it is to *live*.'

'Mary is very interesting,' sighed Lesbia; 'but I fear she was not a correct person.'

'My love, what correct person ever is interesting! History draws a misty halo round a sinner of that kind, till one almost believes her a saint. I think Mary Stuart, Froude's Mary, simply perfect.'

Lesbia had begun by blushing at Lady Kirkbank's opinions; but she was now used to the audacity of the lady's sentiments, and the almost infantile candour with which she gave utterance to them. Lady Kirkbank liked to make her friends laugh. It was all she could do now in order to be admired. And there is nothing like audacity for making people laugh now-a-days. Lady Kirkbank was a close student of all those delightful books of French memoirs which bring the tittle-tattle of the Regency and the scandals of Louis the Fifteenth's reign so vividly before us: and she had unconsciously founded her manners and her ways of thinking and talking upon that easy-going but elegant age. She did not want to seem better than women who had been so altogether charming. She fortified the frivolity of historical Parisian manners by a dash of the British sporting character. She drove, shot, jumped over five-barred gates, contrived on the verge of seventy to be as active as a young woman; and she flattered herself that the mixture of wit, audacity, sport, and good-nature was full of fascination.

However this might be, it is certain that a good many people liked her, chiefly perhaps because she was good-natured, and a little on account of that admirable cook.

To Lesbia, who had been weary to loathing of her old life amidst the hills and waterfalls of Westmoreland, this new life was one perpetual round of pleasure. She flung herself with all her heart and mind into the amusement of the moment; she knew neither weariness nor satiety. To ride in the park in the morning, to go to a luncheon party, a garden party, to drive in the park for half an hour after the garden party, to rush home and dress for the fourth or fifth time, and then off to a dinner, and from dinner to drum, and from drum to big ball, at which rumour said the Prince and Princess were to be present; and so, from eleven o'clock in the morning till four or five o'clock next morning, the giddy whirl went on: and every hour was so occupied by pleasure engagements that it was difficult to squeeze in an occasional morning for shopping—necessary to go to the shops sometimes, or one would not know how many things one really wants—or for an indispensable interview with the dressmaker.

Those mornings at the shops were hardly the least agreeable of Lesbia's hours. To a girl brought up in one perpetual *tête-à-tête* with green hill-sides and silvery watercourses, the West End shops were as gardens of Eden, as Aladdin Caves, as anything, everything that is rapturous and intoxicating. Lesbia, the clear-headed, the cold-hearted, fairly lost her senses when she went into one of those exquisite shops, where a confusion of brocades and satins lay about in dazzling masses of richest colour, with here and there a bunch of lilies, a cluster of roses, a tortoise-shell fan, an ostrich feather, or a flounce of peerless Point d'Alençon flung carelessly athwart the sheen of a wine-dark velvet or golden-hued satin.

Lady Maulevrier had said Lesbia was to have *carte blanche*; so Lesbia bought everything she wanted, or fancied she wanted, or that the shop-people thought she must want, or that Lady Kirkbank happened to admire. The shop-people were so obliging, and so deeply obliged by Lesbia's patronage. She was exactly the kind of customer they liked to serve. She flitted about their showrooms like a beautiful butterfly hovering over a flower-bed—her eye caught by every novelty. She never asked the price of anything: and Lady Kirkbank informed them, in confidence, that she was a great heiress, with a millionaire grandmother who indulged her every whim. Other high-born young ladies, shopping upon fixed allowances, and sorely perplexed to make both ends meet, looked with eyes of envy upon this girl.

And then came the visit to the dressmaker. It happened after all that Kate Kearney was not intrusted with Lady Lesbia's frocks. Miss Kearney was the fashion, and could pick and choose her customers; and as she was a young lady of good business aptitudes, she had a liking for ready money, or at least half-yearly settlements; and, finding that Lady Kirkbank was much more willing to give new orders than to pay old accounts, she had respectfully informed her lady-ship that a pressure of business would prevent

her executing any further commands from Arlington Street, while the necessity of posting her
ledger obliged her to request the favour of an
immediate cheque.

This little skirmish—per letter—occurred while
Lady Kirkbank was at Cannes, and Miss
Kearney's conduct was stigmatised as insolent
and ungrateful, since had not she, Lady Kirkbank
by the mere fact of her patronage, given this
young person her chief claim to fashion?

'I shall drop her,' said Georgie, 'and go back
to poor old Seraphine, who is worth a cartload
of such Irish adventuresses.'

So to Madame Seraphine, of Clanricarde Place,
Lady Lesbia was taken as a lamb to the slaughter-
house.

Seraphine had made Lady Kirkbank's clothes,
off and on, for the last thirty years. Seraphine
and Georgie had grown old together. Lady Kirkbank was always dropping Seraphine and taking
her up again, quarrelling and making friends with
her. They wrote each other little notes, in which
Lady Kirkbank called the dressmaker her *cher*

ange—her *bonne chatte*, her *chère vielle sotte*—and all manner of affectionate names—and in which Seraphine occasionally threatened the lady with the dire engines of the law, if money were not forthcoming before Saturday evening.

Lady Kirkbank within those thirty years had paid Seraphine many thousands; but she had never once got herself out of the dear creature's debt. All her payments were payments on account. A hundred pounds; or fifty—or an occasional cheque for two hundred and fifty, when Sir George had been lucky at Newmarket and Doncaster. But the rolling nucleus of debt went rolling on, growing bigger every year, until the payments on account needed to be larger or more numerous than of old to keep Seraphine in good humour.

Seraphine was a woman of genius and versatility, and had more than one art at her fingers' ends—those skinny and claw-shaped fingers, the nails whereof were not always clean. She took charge of her customer's figures, and made their corsets, and lectured them if they allowed nature to get the upper hand.

'If Madame's waist gets one quarter of an inch thicker it must be that I renounce to make her gowns,' she would tell a ponderous matron, with cool insolence, and the matron would stand abashed before the little sallow, hook-nosed, keen-eyed Jewess, like a child before a severe mother.

'Oh, Seraphine, do you really think that I am stouter?' the customer would ask feebly, panting in her tightened corset.

'Is it that I think so? Why, that jumps to the eyes. Madame had always that little air of Rubens, even in the flower of her youth—but now—it is a Rubens of the Faubourg du Temple.'

And horrified at the idea of her vulgarised charms the meek matron would consent to encase herself in one of Seraphine's severest corsets, called in bitterest mockery *à la santé*—at five guineas—in order that the dressmaker might measure her for a forty-guinea gown.

'A plain satin gown, my dear, with an eighteenpenny frilling round the neck and sleeves, and not so much trimming as would go round my little finger. It is positive robbery,' the matron told her friends afterwards, not the less proud of her skin-tight high-shouldered sleeves and the peerless flow of her train.

Seraphine was an artist in complexions, and it was she who provided her middle-aged and elderly customers with the lilies and roses of youth. Lady Kirkbank's town complexion was superintended by Seraphine, sometimes even manipulated by those harpy-like claws. The eyebrows of which Lesbia complained were only eyebrows *de province* —eyebrows *de voyage*. In London Georgie was much more particular; and Seraphine was often in Arlington Street with her little morocco bag of washes and creams, and brushes and sponges, to prepare Lady Kirkbank for some great party, and to instruct Lady Kirkbank's maid. At such times Georgie was all affection for the little dressmaker.

'*Ma chatte*, you have made me positively adorable,' she would say, peering at her reflection in the ivory hand-mirror, a dazzling image of rouge and bismuth, carmined lips, diamonds, and frizzy yellow hair; 'I verily believe I look under thirty —but do not you think this gown is a thought too *decolletée—un peu trop de peau, hein?*'

'Not for you, Lady Kirkbank, with your fine shoulders. Shoulders are of no age—*les épaules sont la vraie fontaine de jouvence pour les jolies femmes.*

'You are such a witty creature, Seraphine, Fifine. You ought to be a descendant of that wicked old Madame du Deffand. Rilboche, give Madame some more chartreuse.'

And Lady Kirkbank and the dressmaker would chink their liqueur glasses in amity before the lady gathered up her satin train and allowed her peerless shoulders to be muffled in a plush mantle to go down to her carriage, fortified by that last glass of green chartreuse.

There were always the finest chartreuse and curaçoa in a liqueur cabinet on Lady Kirkbank's dressing-table. The cabinet formed a companion to the dressing-case, which contained all those creamy and rose-hued cosmetics, powders, brushes, and medicaments, which were necessary for the manufacture of Georgie's complexion. The third bottle in the liqueur case held cognac, and this, as Rilboche the maid knew, was oftenest replenished. Yet nobody could accuse Lady Kirkbank of intemperate habits. The liqueur box only supplied the peg that was occasionally wanted to screw the superior mind to concert pitch.

'One must always be at concert pitch in society, don't you know, my dear,' said Georgie to her young *protégée*.

Thus it happened that, Miss Kearney having behaved badly, Lesbia was carried off to dear old Seraphine, and delivered over to that modern witch, as a sacrifice tied to the horns of the altar.

Clanricarde Place is a little nook of Queen Anne houses—genuine Queen Anne, be it understood—between Piccadilly and St. James's Palace, and hardly five minutes' walk from Arlington Street. It is a quiet little *cul de sac* in the very heart of the fashionable world; and here of an afternoon might be seen the carriages of Madame Seraphine's customers, blocking the whole of the carriage way, and choking up the narrow entrance to the street, which widened considerably at the inner end.

Madame Seraphine's house was at the end, a narrow house, with tall old-fashioned windows curtained with amber satin. It was a small, dark house, and exhaled occasional odours of garlic and main sewer : but the staircase was a gem in old oak, and the furniture in the triple telescopic drawing-rooms, dwindling to a closet at the end, was genuine Louis Seize.

Seraphine herself was the only shabby thing in the house—a wizened little woman, with a wicked old Jewish face, and one shoulder higher than the other, dressed in a shiny black moire gown, years after moires had been exploded, and with a rag of old lace upon her sleek black hair—raven black hair, and the only good thing about her appearance.

One ornament, and one only, had Seraphine ever been guilty of wearing, and that was an old-fashioned half-hoop ring of Brazilian diamonds, brilliants of the first water. This ring she called her yard measure; and she was in the habit of using it as her standard of purity, and comparing it with any diamonds which her customers submitted to her inspection. For the clever little dressmaker had a feeling heart for a lady in difficulties, and was in the habit of lending money on good security, and on terms that were almost reasonable as compared with the usurious rates one reads of in the newspapers.

Lesbia's first sensation upon having this accomplished person presented to her was one of shrinking and disgust. There was something sinister in the sallow face, the small shrewd eyes, and long hooked nose, the crooked figure, and claw-shaped hands. But when Madame Seraphine began to talk about gowns, and bade her acolytes— smartly-dressed young women with pleasing countenances—bring forth marvels of brocade and satin, embroideries, stamped velvets, bullion fringes, and ostrich feather flouncings, Lesbia became interested, and forgot the unholy aspect of the high priestess.

Lady Kirkbank and the dressmaker discussed

Lesbia's charms as calmly as if she had been out of the room.

'What do you think of her figure?' asked Lady Kirkbank.

'One cannot criticise what does not exist,' replied the dressmaker, in French. 'The young lady has no figure. She has evidently been brought up in the country.'

And then with rapid bird-like movements, and with her head on one side, Seraphine measured Lesbia's waist and bust, muttering little argotic expressions *sotto voce* as she did so.

'Waist three inches too large, shoulders six inches too narrow,' she said decisively, and she dictated some figures to one of the damsels, who wrote them down in an order-book.

'What does that mean?' asked Lesbia, not at all approving of such cavalier treatment.

'Only that Seraphine will make your corsets the right size,' answered Lady Kirkbank.

'What? Three inches too small for my waist, and six too wide for my shoulders?'

'My love, you must have a figure,' replied

Lady Kirkbank, conclusively. 'It is not what you are, but what you ought to be that has to be considered.'

So Lesbia, the cool-headed, who was also the weak-minded, consented to have her figure adjusted to the regulation mark of absolute beauty, as understood by Madame Seraphine. It was only when her complexion came under discussion, and Seraphine ventured to suggest that she would be all the better for a little accentuation of her eyebrows and darkening of her lashes, that Lesbia made a stand.

'What would my grandmother think of me if she heard I painted?' she asked, indignantly.

Lady Kirkbank laughed at her *naïveté*.

'My dear child, your grandmother is just half a century behind the age,' she said. 'I hope you are not going to allow your life in London to be regulated by an oracle at Grasmere?'

'I am not going to paint my face,' replied Lesbia, firmly.

'Well, perhaps you are right. The eyebrows are a little weak and undecided, Seraphine, as you say, and the lashes would be all the better for your famous cosmetic; but after all there is a charm in what the painters call "sincerity," and any little errors of detail will prove the genuineness of Lady Lesbia's beauty. One *may* be too artistic.'

And Lady Kirkbank gave a complacent glance at her own image in one of the Marie Antoinette mirrors, pleased with the general effect of arched brows, darkened eyelids, and a daisy bonnet. The fair Georgie generally affected field-flowers and other simplicities, which would have been becoming to a beauty of eighteen.

'One is obliged to smother one's self in satin and velvet for balls and dinners,' said Lady Kirkbank, when she discussed the great question of gowns; 'but I know I always look my best in my cotton frock and straw hat.'

That first visit to Seraphine's den—den as terrible, did one but know it, as that antediluvian hyena-cave at Torquay, where the threshold is worn by the bodies of beasts dragged across it, and the ground paved with their bones — that

first visit was a serious business. Later interviews might be mere frivolities, half-an-hour wasted
in looking at new fashions, an order given carelessly on the spur of the moment : but upon this
occasion Lady Kirkbank had to arm her young
protégée for the coming compaign, and the question
was to the last degree serious.

The chaperon and the dressmaker put their
heads together, looked at fashion plates, talked
solemnly of Worth and his compeers, of the gowns
that were being worn by Bernhardt, and Pierson,
and Croisette, and other stars of the Parisian
stage : and then Lady Kirkbank gave her orders,
Lesbia listening and assenting.

Nothing was said about prices ; but Lesbia
had a vague idea that some of the things would
be rather expensive, and she ventured to ask
Lady Kirkbank if she were not ordering too many
gowns.

'My dear, Lady Maulevrier said you were
to have *carte blanche*,' replied Georgie, solemnly.
'Your dear grandmother is as rich as Crœsus,
and she is generosity itself ; and how should I

ever forgive myself if I allowed you to appear in society in an inadequate style. You have to take a high place, the very highest place, Lesbia ; and you must be dressed in accordance with that position.'

Lesbia said no more. After all it was Lady Kirkbank's business and not hers. She had been entrusted to Lady Kirkbank as to a person who thoroughly knew the great world, and she must submit to be governed by the wisdom and ex-perience of her chaperon. If the bills were heavy, that would be Lady Kirkbank's affair ; and no doubt dear grandmother was rich enough to afford anything Lesbia wanted. She had been told that she was to take rank among heiresses.

Lady Maulevrier had given her granddaughter some old-fashioned ornaments, topaz, amethysts, turquoise—jewels that had belonged to dead and gone Talmashes and Angersthorpes—to be reset. This entailed a visit to a Bond Street jeweller, and in the dazzling glass-cases on the counter of the Bond Street establishment Lesbia saw a good many things which she felt were real necessities to her new phase of existence, and these, with Lady Kirkbank's **approval**, she **ordered**. They were not important matters. Half-a-dozen gold bangles of real oriental workmanship, three or four jewelled **arrows, flies** and beetles, and cater-pillars, **to pin on her** laces and flowers, a diamond clasp for her pearl necklace, a dear little gold hunter to wear when she rode in the park, a diamond butterfly to light up that old-fashioned amethyst *parure* which the **jeweller was to reset with an artistic** admixture of brilliants.

'I am sure you would not like the effect without diamonds,' said the jeweller. 'Your amethysts are very fine, but they are dark and heavy in tone, and want a good deal of lighting up, especially for the present fashion of half-lighted rooms. If you will allow me to use my own discretion, and mix in a few brilliants, I shall be able to produce a really artistic *parure;* otherwise I would not recommend you to touch them. The present setting is clumsy and inelegant; but I really do not know that I could improve upon it, without an admixture of brilliants.'

'Will the diamonds add very much to the expense?' Lesbia inquired, timidly.

'My dear child, you are perfectly safe in leaving the matter in Mr. Cabochon's hands,' interposed Lady Kirkbank, who had particular reasons for wishing to be on good terms with the head of the establishment. 'Your dear grandmother gave you the amethysts to be reset; and of course she would wish it to be done in an artistic manner. Otherwise, as Mr. Cabochon judiciously says, why have the stones reset at all? Better wear them in all their present hideousness.'

Of course, after this Lesbia consented to the amethysts being dealt with according to Mr. Cabochon's taste.

'Which is simply perfect,' interjected Lady Kirkbank.

And now Lesbia's campaign began in real earnest—a life of pleasure, a life of utter selfishness and self-indulgence, which would go far to pervert the strongest mind, to tarnish the purest nature. To dress and be admired—that was what Lesbia's life meant from morning till night. She had no higher or nobler aim. Even on Sunday mornings at the fashionable church, where the women sat on one side of the nave and the men on the other, where divinest music was as a pair of wings, on which the enraptured soul flew heavenward—even here Lesbia thought more of her bonnet and her gloves—the *chic* or non-*chic* of her whole costume, than of the service. She might kneel gracefully, with her bent head, just revealing the ivory whiteness of a lovely throat, between the edge of her lace frilling and the flowers in her bonnet. She might look the fairest image of devotion; but how could a woman pray whose heart was a milliner's shop, whose highest ambition was to be prettier and better dressed than other women?

The season was six weeks old. It was Ascot week, the crowning glory of the year, and Lesbia and her chaperon had secured tickets for the Royal enclosure—or it may be said rather that Lesbia had secured them—for the Master of the Royal Buckhounds might have omitted poor old Lady Kirkbank's familiar name from his list if it had not been for that lovely girl who went everywhere under the veteran's wing.

Six weeks, and Lesbia's appearance in society had been one perpetual triumph; but as yet nothing serious had happened. She had had no offers. Half a dozen men had tried their hardest to propose to her—had sat out dances, had waylaid her in conservatories and in back drawing-rooms, in lobbies while she waited for her carriage—had looked at her piteously with tenderest declarations trembling on their lips; but she had contrived to keep them at bay, to strike them dumb by her coldness, or confound them by her coquetry: for all these were ineligibles, whom Lady Lesbia Haselden did not want to have the trouble of refusing.

Lady Kirkbank was in no haste to marry her *protégée*—nay, it was much more to her interest that Lesbia should remain single for three or four seasons, and that she, Lady Kirkbank, might have the advantage of close association with the young beauty, and the privilege of spending Lady Maulevrier's money. But she would have liked to be able to inform Lesbia's grandmother of some tremendous conquest—the subjugation of a worthy victim. This herd of nobodies—younger sons with courtesy titles and empty pockets, ruined Guardsmen, briefless barristers—what was the use of telling Lady Maulevrier about such barren victories? Lady Kirkbank therefore contented herself with expatiating upon Lesbia's triumphs in a general way: how graciously the Princess spoke to her and about her; how she had been asked to sit on the dais at the ball at Marlborough House, and had danced in the Royal quadrille.

'Has Lesbia happened to meet Lord Hartfield?' Lady Maulevrier, asked, incidentally in one of her letters.

No. Lord Hartfield was in London, for he had made a great speech in the Lords on a question of vital interest; but he was not going into society, or at any rate into society of a frivolous kind. He had given himself up to politics, as so many young men did nowadays, which was altogether horrid of them. His name had appeared in the list of guests at one or two cabinet dinners; but the world of polo matches and afternoon teas, dances and drums, private theatricals, and Orleans House suppers, knew him not. As a competitor on the fashionable racecourse, Lord Hartfield was, in common parlance, out of the running.

And now on this glorious June day, this Thursday of Thursdays, the Ascot Cup day, for the first time since Lesbia's *début*, Lady Kirkbank had occasion to smile upon an admirer whose pretensions were worthy of the highest consideration.

Mr. Smithson, of Park Lane, and Rood Hall, near Henley, and Formosa, Cowes, and Le Bouge, Deauville, and a good many other places too numerous to mention, was reputed to be one of the richest commoners in England. He was a man of that uncertain period of life which enemies call middle age, and friends call youth. That he would never see a five-and-thirtieth birthday again was certain; but whether he had passed the Rubicon of forty was open to doubt. It is possible that he was enjoying those few golden years between thirty-five and forty, which for the wealthy bachelor constitute verily the prime and summer-tide of life. Wisdom has come, experience has been bought, taste has been cultivated, the man has educated himself to the uttermost in the great school of daily life. He knows his world thoroughly, whatever that world is, and he knows how to enjoy every gift and every advantage which Providence has bestowed upon him.

Mr. Smithson was a great authority on the Stock Exchange, though he had ceased for the last three or four years to frequent the 'House,' or to be seen in the purlieus of Throgmorton Street. Indeed he had an air of harldly knowing his way to the City, of being acquainted with that part of London only by hearsay. He complained that his horses shied at passing Temple Bar. And yet a few years ago Mr. Smithson's city operations had been on a very extensive scale. It was in the rise and fall of commodities rather than of stocks and shares that Horace Smithson had made his money. He had exercised occult influences upon the trade of the great city, of the world itself, whereof that city is in a manner the keystone. Iron had risen or fallen at his

beck.   At the breath of his nostrils cochineal had
gone up in the market at an almost magical rate,
as if the whole civilised world had become suddenly
intent upon dyeing its garments red, nay, as if
even the naked savages of the Gold Coast and the
tribes of Central Africa were bent on staining
their dusky skins with the bodies of the female
coccus.

Favoured by a hint from Smithson, his
particular friends followed his lead, and rushed
into the markets to buy all the cochineal
that could be had; to buy at any price, since the
market was rising hourly.   And then, all in a
moment, as the sky clouds over on a summer day,
there came a dulness in the cochineal market,
and the female coccus was being sold at an
enormous sacrifice.   And anon it leaked out that
Mr. Smithson had grown tired of cochineal, and
had been selling for the last week or two: and
it was noised abroad that this rise and fall in
cocci had brought Mr. Smithson seventy thousand
pounds.

Mr. Smithson was said to have commenced

life in a very humble capacity. There were some
who declared he was the very youth who stooped
to pick up a pin in a Parisian banker's courtyard, after **his services** as clerk had just been
rejected by the firm, **and who** was thereupon
recognised as a youth **worthy of favour and taken**
into the banker's office. But this touching
incident **of the pin was too** ancient a tradition **to**
fit Mr. Smithson, still under forty.

Some there were who remembered him eighteen
years ago as an adventurer in the great wilderness
of London, penniless, friendless, a Jack-of-all-
trades, **living as** the birds **of the air live, and**
with **as** little certainty of **future maintenance.**
And then Mr. Smithson disappeared for a space—
he went **under, as** his friends called it ; **to re-**
appear **fifteen years later as** Smithson **the**
millionaire. He had been in Peru, Mexico,
California. He had traded in hides, in diamonds,
in silver, in stocks and shares. And now he was
the great Smithson, whose voice **was the voice of**
an oracle, who **was** supposed **to be** able **to make**
the fortunes of other men by a word or a wink,

a nod, or a little look across the crowd, and whom all the men and women in London society —short of that exclusive circle which does *not* open its ranks to Smithsons—were ready to cherish and admire.

Mr. Smithson had been in Petersburg, Paris, Vienna, all over civilised Europe during the last five weeks, whether on business or on pleasure bent, nobody knew. He affected to be an elegant idler ; but it was said by the initiated that wherever Smithson went the markets rose or fell, and hides iron, copper, or tin, felt the influence of his presence.

He came back to London in time for the Cup Day, and in time to fall desperately in love with Lesbia, whom he met for the first time in the Royal enclosure.

She was dressed in white, purest ivory white, from top to toe — radiant, dazzling, under an immense sunshade fringed with creamy marabouts. Her complexion—untouched by Seraphine—her dark and glossy hair, her large violet eyes, luminous, dark almost to blackness, were all set off and accentuated by the absence of colour in her costume. Even the cluster of exotics on her shoulder were of the same pure tint, gardenias and lilies of the valley.

Mr. Smithson was formally presented to the new beauty, and received with a cool contempt which riveted his chains. He was so accustomed to be run after by women that it was a new sensation to meet one who was not in the least impressed by his superior merits.

' I don't suppose the girl knows who I am,' he said to himself, for although he had a very good idea of his intrinsic worth, he knew that his wealth ranked first among his merits.

But on after occasions when Lesbia had been told all that could be told to the advantage of Mr. Smithson, she accepted his homage with the same indifference, and treated him with less favour than she accorded to the ruined guardsmen and younger sons who were dying for her.

CHAPTER VIII.

IT was a Saturday afternoon, and even in that great world which has no occupation in life except to amuse itself, whose days are all holidays, there is a sort of exceptional flavour, a kind of extra excitement on Saturday afternoons, distinguished by polo matches at Hurlingham, just as Saturday evenings are by the production of new plays at fashionable theatres. There was a great military polo match for this particular Saturday—Lancers against Dragoons. It was a lovely June afternoon, and Hurlingham would be at its best. The cool greensward, the branching trees, the flowing river would afford an unspeakable relief after the block of carriages in Bond Street and the heated air of London, where even the parks felt baked and arid; and to Hurlingham Lady Kirkbank drove directly after luncheon.

Lesbia leaned back in the barouche listening calmly, while her chaperon expatiated upon the wealth and possessions of Horace Smithson. It was now ten days since the meeting at Ascot, and Mr. Smithson had contrived to see a great deal of Lesbia in that short time. He was invited almost everywhere, and he had haunted her at afternoon and evening parties; he had supped in Arlington Street after the opera; he had played cards with Lesbia, and had enjoyed the felicity of winning her money. His admiration was obvious, and there was a seriousness in his manner of pursuing her which showed that, in Lady Kirkbank's unromantic phraseology, 'the man meant business.'

'Smithson is caught at last, and I am glad of it,' said Georgie. 'The creature is an abominable flirt, and has broken more hearts than any man in London. He was all but the death of one of the dearest girls I know.'

'Mr. Smithson break hearts!' exclaimed Lesbia,

languidly. 'I should not have thought that was in his line. Mr. Smithson is not an Adonis, nor are his manners particularly fascinating.'

'My child, how fresh you are! Do you suppose it is the handsome men or the fascinating men for whom women break their hearts in society? It is the rich men they all want to marry—men like Smithson, who can give them diamonds, and yachts, and a hunting stud, and half a dozen fine houses. Those are the prizes—the blue ribbons of the matrimonial racecourse—men like Smithson, who pretend to admire all the pretty women, who dangle, and dangle, and dangle, and keep off other offers, and give ten guinea bouquets, and then at the end of the season are off to Hombourg or the Scotch moors, without a word. Do you think that kind of treatment is not hard enough to break a penniless girl's heart? She sees the golden prize within her grasp, as she believes; she thinks that she and poverty have parted company for ever; she imagines herself mistress of town house and country houses, yachts and stables; and then one fine morning the gentleman is off and away! Do not you think that is enough to break a girl's heart?'

'I can imagine that a girl steeped to the lips in poverty might be willing to marry Mr. Smithson's houses and yachts,' answered Lesbia in her low, sweet voice, with a faint sneer even amidst the sweetness, 'but I think it must have been a happy release for any one to be let off the sacrifice at the last moment.'

'Poor Belle Trinder did not think so.'

'Who was Belle Trinder?'

'An Essex parson's daughter whom I took under my wing five years ago—a splendid girl, large and fair, and just a trifle coarse—not to be spoken of in the same day with you, dearest; but still a decidedly handsome creature. And she took remarkably well. She was a very lively girl, "never ran mute," Sir George used to say. Sir George was very fond of her. She amused him, poor girl, with her rather brainless rattle.'

'And Mr. Smithson admired her?'

'Followed her about everywhere, sent her whole flower gardens in the way of bouquets and

Japanese baskets, and floral *parures* for her gowns, and opera boxes and concert tickets. Their names were always coupled. People used to call them Bel and the Dragon. The poor child made up her mind she was to be Mrs. Smithson. She used to talk of what she would do for her own people—the poor old father, buried alive in a damp parsonage, and struggling every winter with chronic bronchitis; the four younger sisters pining in dulness and penury; the mother who hardly knew what it was to rest from the continual worries of daily life.'

'Poor things!' sighed Lesbia, gazing admiringly at the handle of her last new sunshade.

'Belle used to talk of what she would do for them all,' pursued Lady Kirkbank. 'Father should go every year to the villa at Monte Carlo; mother and the girls should have a month in Park Lane every season, and their autumn holiday at one of Mr. Smithson's country houses. I knew the world well enough to be sure that this kind of thing would never answer with a man like Smithson. It is only one man in a thousand—

the modern Arthur, the modern Quixote—who will marry a whole family. I told Belle as much, but she laughed. She felt so secure of her power over the man. "He will do anything I ask him," she said.'

'Miss Trinder must be an extraordinary young person,' observed Lesbia, scornfully. 'The man had not proposed, had he?'

'No, the actual proposal hung fire, but Belle thought it was a settled thing all the same. Everybody talked to her as if she were engaged to Smithson, and those poor, ignorant vicarage girls used to write her long letters of congratulation, envying her good fortune, speculating about what she would do when she was married. The girl was too open and candid for London society —talked too much, "gave the view before she was sure of her fox," Sir George said. All this silly talk came to Smithson's ears, and one morning we read in the 'Post' that Mr. Smithson had started the day before for Algiers, where he was to stay at the house of the English Consul, and hunt lions. We waited all day, hoping for some letter of explanation, some friendly farewell which would mean *à revoir*. But there was nothing; and then poor Belle gave way altogether. She shut herself up in her room, and went out of one hysterical fit into another. I never heard a girl sob so terribly. She was not fit to be seen for a week, and then she went home to her father's parsonage in the flat, swampy country on the borders of Suffolk, and eat her heart, as Byron calls it. And the worst of it was that she had no actual justification for considering herself jilted. She had talked, and other people had talked, and among them they had settled the business. But Smithson had said hardly anything. He had only flirted to his heart's content, and had spent a few hundreds upon flowers, gloves, fans, and opera tickets, which perhaps would not have been accepted by a girl with a strong sense of her own dignity.'

'I should think not, indeed,' interjected Lesbia.

'But which poor Belle was only too delighted to get.'

. Miss Trinder must be very bad style,' said

Lesbia, with languid scorn, 'and Mr. Smithson is an execrable person. Did she die?'

'No, my dear, she is alive, poor soul!'

'You said he broke her heart.'

'"The heart may break, yet brokenly live on,"' quoted Lady Kirkbank. 'The disappointed young women don't all die. They take to district visiting, or rational dressing, or china painting, or an ambulance brigade. The lucky ones marry well-to-do widowers with large families, and so slip into a comfortable groove by the time they are five-and-thirty. Poor Belle is still single, still buried in the damp parsonage, where she paints plates and teacups, and wears out my old gowns, just as she is wearing out her own life, poor creature!'

'The idea of any one wanting to marry Mr. Smithson,' said Lesbia. 'It seems too dreadful.'

'A case of real destitution, you think. Wait till you have seen Smithson's house in Park Lane—his team, his yacht, his orchid houses in Berkshire.'

Lesbia sighed. Her knowledge of London

society was only seven weeks old; and yet already the day of disenchantment had begun! She was having her eyes opened to the stern realities of life. A year ago when her appearance in the great world was still only a dream of the future, she had pictured to herself the crowd of suitors who would come to woo, and she had resolved to choose the worthiest.

What would he be like, that worthiest among the wooers, that King Arthur among her knights?

First and foremost, he would be of rank higher than her own—a duke, a marquis, or one of the first and oldest among earls. Title and lofty lineage were indispensable. It would be a fall, a failure, a disappointment, were she to marry a commoner, however distinguished.

The worthy one must be noble, therefore, and of the old nobility. He must be young, handsome, intellectual. He must stand out from among his peers by his gifts of mind and person. He must have won distinction in the arena of politics or diplomacy, arms or letters. He must be 'somebody,'

She had been seven weeks in society, and this modern Arthur had not appeared. So far as she had been able to discover, there was no such person. The dukes and marquises were mostly men of advanced years. The young unmarried nobility were given over to sport, play, and foolishness. She had heard of only one man who at all corresponded with her ideal, and he was Lord Hartfield. But Lord Hartfield had given himself up to politics, and was no doubt a prig. Lady Kirkbank spoke of him with contempt, as an intolerable person. But then Lord Hartfield was not in Lady Kirkbank's set. He belonged to that serious circle to which Lady Kirkbank's house appeared about as reputable a place of gathering as a booth on a racecourse.

And now Lady Kirkbank told Lesbia that this Mr. Smithson, a nobody with a great fortune, was a man whose addresses she, the sister of Lord Maulevrier, ought to welcome. Mr. Smithson, who claimed to be a lineal descendant of that Sir Michael Carrington, standard-bearer to Cœur de Lion in the Holy Land, whose descendants changed their name to Smith during the Wars of the Roses. Mr. Smithson boldly proclaimed himself a scion of this good old county family, and bore on his plate and his coach panels the elephant’s head and the three demi-griffins of the Hertfordshire Smiths, who only smiled and shrugged their shoulders when they were complimented upon the splendid surroundings of their cousin. Who could tell? Some lateral branch of the standard-bearer’s family tree might have borne this illustrious twig.·

Lady Kirkbank and all Lady Kirkbank’s friends seemed to have conspired to teach Lesbia Haselden one lesson, and that lesson meant that money was the first prize in the great game of life. Money ranked before everything—before titles, before noble lineage, genius, fame, beauty, courage, honour. Money was Alpha and Omega, the beginning and the end. Mr. Smithson, whose antecedents were as cloudy as those of Aphrodite, was a greater man than a peer whose broad acres only brought him two per cent., or half of whose farms were tenantless, and his fields growing cockle instead of barley.

Yes, Lady Lesbia's illusions were reft from her one by one. A year ago she had fancied beauty all-powerful, a gift which must ensure to its possessor dominion over all the kingdoms of the earth. Rank, intellect, fame would bow down before that magical diadem. And, behold, she had been shining upon London society for seven weeks, and only empty heads and empty pockets had bowed down — the frivolous, the ineligible, —and Mr. Smithson.

Another illusion which had been dispelled was Lesbia's comfortable idea of her own expectations. Her grandmother had told her that she might take rank among heiresses; and she had held herself accordingly, deeming that her place was among the wealthiest. And now, since Mr. Smithson's appearance upon the scene, Lady Kirkbank had informed her young friend with noble candour that Lady Maulevrier's fortune, however large it might seem at Grasmere, would be a poor thing in London; and that Lady Maulevrier's ideas about money were as old-fashioned as her notions about morals.

'Life is about six times as expensive as it was in your grandmother's time,' said Lady Kirkbank, as the carriage rolled softly along the shabby road between Knightsbridge and Fulham. 'It is the pace that kills. Society, which used to jog along comfortably, like the old Brighton stage, at ten miles an hour, now goes as fast as the Brighton express. In my mother's time poor Lord Byron was held up to the execration of respectable people as the type of cynical profligacy; in my own time people talked about Lord Waterford; but, my dear, the young men now are all Byrons and Waterfords, without the genius of the one or the generosity of the other. We are all going at steeplechase rate. Social success without money is impossible. The rich Americans, the successful Jews, will crowd us out unless we keep pace with them. Ah, Lesbia, my dear girl, there would be a great future before you if you could only make up your mind to accept Mr. Smithson.'

'How do you know that he means to propose to me?' asked Lesbia mockingly. 'Perhaps he is only going to behave as he did to Miss Trinder.'

'Lady Lesbia Haselden is a very different person from a country parson's daughter,' answered her chaperon; 'Smithson told me all about it afterwards. He was really taken with Belle's showy good looks; but one of her particular friends told him of her foolish talk about her sisters, and how well she meant to get them married when she was Mrs. Smithson. This disgusted him. He went down to Essex, reconnoitered the parsonage, saw one of the sisters hanging out cuffs and collars in the orchard—another feeding the fowls—both in shabby gowns and country-made boots; one of them with red hair and freckles. The mother was bargaining for fish with a hawker at the kitchen door. And these were the people he was expected to import into Park Lane, under ceilings painted by Leighton. These were the people he was to exhibit on board his yacht, to cart about on his drag. "I had half made up my mind to marry the girl, but I would sooner have hung myself than marry her mother and sisters, so I took the first train for Paris, en route to Algiers," said Smithson, and upon my word I could hardly blame the man,' concluded Lady Kirkbank.

They were driving up the narrow avenue to the gates of Hurlingham by this time. Lesbia shook out her frock and looked at her gloves, tan-coloured mousquetaires, reaching up to the elbow, and embroidered to match her frock.

To-day she was a study in brown and gold. Brown satin petticoat embroidered with marsh marigolds ; little bronze shoes, with marsh marigolds tied on the lachets ; brown stockings with marsh marigold clocks ; tunic brown foulard smothered with quillings of soft brown lace ; Princess bonnet of brown straw, with a wreath of marsh marigold and a neat little buckle of brown diamonds ; parasol brown satin, with an immense bunch of marsh marigolds on the top, fan to match parasol.

The seats in front of the field were nearly all full when Lady Kirkbank and Lesbia left their carriage ; but their interests had been protected by a gentleman who had turned down two chairs and sat between them on guard. This was Mr. Smithson.

'I have been sitting here for an hour keeping your chairs,' he said, as he rose to greet them. 'You have no idea what work I have had, and how suspiciously all the women have looked at me.'

The match was going on. The Lancers scuffling for the ball—a fine display of hog-maned ponies and close-cropped young men in ideal boots. But Lesbia cared very little about the match. She was looking along the serried ranks of youth and beauty to see if anybody's costume was smarter than her own.

No. She could see nothing she liked so well as her brown satin and buttercups. She sat down in a perfectly contented frame of mind, pleased with herself and with Seraphine — pleased even with Mr. Smithson, who had shown himself devoted by his patient attendance upon the empty chairs.

After the match was over the two ladies and their attendant strolled about the gardens. Other men came and fluttered round Lesbia, and women and girls exchanged endearing smiles and pretty little words of greeting with her, and envied her the brown frock and buttercups and Mr. Smithson at her chariot wheel. And then they went to the lawn in front of the club-house, which was so crowded that even Mr. Smithson found it difficult to get a tea-table, and would hardly have succeeded so soon as he did if it had not been for the assistance of a couple of Lesbia's devoted Guardsmen, who ran to and fro and badgered the waiters.

After much skirmishing they were seated at a rustic table, the blue river gleaming and glancing in the distance, the good old trees spreading their broad shadows over the grass, the company crowding and chattering and laughing—an animated picture of pretty faces, smart gowns, big parasols, Japanese fans.

Lesbia poured out the tea with the prettiest air of domesticity.

'Can you really pour out tea?' gasped a callow lieutenant, gazing upon her with goggling, enraptured eyes. 'I did not think you could do anything so earthly.'

'I can, and drink it too,' answered Lesbia, laughing. 'I adore tea. Cream and sugar?'

'I—I beg your pardon—how many ?' murmured the youth, who had lost himself in gazing, and no longer understood plain English.

Mr. Smithson frowned at the intruder, and contrived to absorb Lesbia's attention for the rest of the afternoon. He had a good deal more to say for himself than her military admirers, and was altogether more amusing. He had a little cynical air which Lesbia's recent education had taught her to enjoy. He depreciated all her female friends—abused their gowns and bonnets, and gave her to understand, between the lines, as it were, that she was the only woman in London worth thinking about.

She looked at him curiously, wondering how Belle Trinder had been able to resign herself to the idea of marrying him.

He was not absolutely bad looking—but he was in all things unlike a girl's ideal lover. He was short and stout, with a pale complexion, and sunken faded eyes, as of a man who had spent the greater part of his life by candle light, and had pored much over ledgers and bank books, share lists and prospectuses. He dressed well, or allowed himself to be dressed by the most correct of tailors — the Prince's tailor — but he never attempted to lead the fashion in his garments. He had no originality. Such sublime flights as that of the man who revived corduroy, or of that daring genius who resuscitated the half-forgotten Inverness coat, were unknown to him. He could only follow the lead of the highest. He had small feet, of which he was intensely proud, podgy white hands on which he wore the most exquisite rings. He changed his rings every day, like a Roman Emperor; was reported to have summer and winter rings — onyx and the coolest looking intaglios set in slenderest filagree for warm weather — fiery rubies and diamonds in massive bands of dull gold for winter. He was said to devote half an hour every morning to the treatment of his nails, which were perfect. All the inkstains of his youth had been obliterated, and those nails which had once been bitten to the quick during the throes of financial study were now things of beauty.

Lady Lesbia surveyed Mr. Smithson critically, and shuddered at the thought that this person was the best substitute which the season had yet offered her for her ideal knight. She thought of John Hammond, the tall, strong figure, straight and square ; the head so proudly carried on a neck which would have graced a Greek arena. The straight, clearly-cut features, the flashing eyes, bright with youth and hope and the promise of all good things. Yes, there was indeed a man— a man in all the nobility of manhood, as God made him, an Adam before the Fall.

Ah, if John Hammond had only possessed a quarter of Mr. Smithson's wealth how gladly would Lesbia have defied the world and married him. But to defy the world upon nothing a year was out of the question.

'Why didn't he go on the Stock Exchange and make his fortune?' thought Lesbia, pettishly, 'instead of talking vaguely about politics and literature.'

She felt angry with her rejected lover for having come to her empty-handed. She had seen no man in London who was, or who seemed to her, his equal. And yet she did not repent of having rejected him. The more she knew of the world and the more she knew of herself the more deeply was she convinced that poverty was an evil thing, and that she was not the right kind of person to endure it.

She was inwardly making these comparisons as they strolled back to the carriage, while Mr. Smithson and Lady Kirkbank talked confidentially at her side.

'Do you know that Lady Kirkbank has promised and vowed three things for you?' said Mr. Smithson.

'Indeed! I thought I was past the age at which one can be compromised by other people's promises. Pray what are those three things?'

'First, that you will come to breakfast in Park Lane with Lady Kirkbank next Wednesday morning. I say Wednesday because that will give me time to ask some nice people to meet you; secondly, that you will honour me by occupying my box at the Lyceum some evening next week ; and thirdly, that you will allow me to drive you down to the Orleans for supper after the play. The drive only takes an hour, and the moonlight nights are delicious at this time of the year.'

' I am i n Lady Kirkbank's hands,' answered Lesbia, laughing. ' I am her goods, her chattels ; she takes me wherever she likes.'

' But would you refuse to do me this honour if you were a free agent ? '

' I can't tell. I hardly know what it is to be a free agent. At Grasmere I did whatever my grandmother told me—in London I obey Lady Kirkbank. I was transferred from one master to another. Why should we breakfast in Park Lane instead of in Arlington Street ? What is the use of crossing Piccadilly to eat our breakfast ? '

This was a cool-headed style of treatment to which Mr. Smithson was not accustomed, and which charmed him accordingly. Young women usually threw themselves at his head, as it were : but here was a girl who talked to him as indifferently as if he were a tradesman offering his wares.

'What a dreadfully practical person you are?' he exclaimed. 'What is the use of crossing Piccadilly? Well, in the first place, you will make me ineffably happy. But perhaps that doesn't count. In the second place, I shall be able to show you some rather good pictures of the French school ——'

'I hate the French school!' interjected Lesbia. 'Tricky, flashy, chalky, shallow, smelling of the footlights and the studio.'

'Well, sink the pictures. You will meet some very charming people, belonging to that artist world which is not to be met everywhere.'

'I will go to Park Lane to meet your people, if Lady Kirkbank likes to take me,' said Lesbia, and with this answer Mr. Smithson was bound to be content.

'My pet, if you had made it the study of your life how to treat that man you could not do it better,' said Lady Kirkbank, when they were driving along the dusty road between dusty hedges and dusty trees, past that last remnant of country which was daily being debased into London. 'Upon my word, Lesbia, I begin to think you must be a genius.'

'Did you see any gowns you liked better than mine?' asked Lesbia, reclining reposefully, with her little bronze shoes upon the opposite cushion.

'Not one—Seraphine has surpassed herself.'

'You are always saying that. One would suppose you were a sleeping partner in the firm. But I really think this brown and buttercups is rather nice. I saw that odious American girl just now—Miss—Miss Milwaukee, that mop-stick girl people raved about at Cannes. She was in pale blue and cream colour, a milk and water mixture, and looked positively plain.'

CHAPTER IX.

LADY KIRKBANK and Lady Lesbia drove across Piccadilly at eleven o'clock on Wednesday morning to breakfast with Mr. Smithson, and although Lesbia had questioned whether it was worth while crossing Piccadilly to eat one's breakfast, she had subsequently considered it worth while ordering a new gown from Seraphine for the occasion; or, it may be, rather that the breakfast made a plausible excuse for a new gown, the pleasure of ordering which was one of those joys of a London life that had not yet lost their savour.

The gown, devised especially for the early morning, was simplicity itself, rusticity even. It was a Dresden shepherdess gown, made of a soft flowered stuff, with roses and forget-me-nots on a creamy ground. There was a great deal of creamy lace, and innumerable yards of palest azure and palest rose ribbon in the confection, and there was a coquettish little hat, the regular Dresden hat, with a wreath of rosebuds.

'Dresden china incarnate!' exclaimed Smithson, as he welcomed Lady Lesbia on the threshold of his marble hall, under the plate-glass marquise which sheltered arrivals at his door. 'Why do you make yourself so lovely? I shall want to keep you in one of my Louis Seize cabinets, with the rest of my Dresden!'

Lady Kirkbank had considered the occasion suitable for one of her favourite cotton frocks and rustic hats—a Leghorn hat, with clusters of dog-roses and honeysuckle, and a trail of the same hedge-flowers to fasten her muslin fichu.

Mr. Smithson's house in Park Lane was simply perfect. It is wonderful what good use a *parvenu* can make of his money nowadays, and how rarely he disgraces himself by any marked offences against good taste. There are so many people at hand to teach the *parvenu* how to furnish his house, or how to choose his stud. If he go wrong it must be by sheer perversity, an arrogant insistance upon being governed by his own ignorant inclinations.

Mr. Smithson was too good a tactician to go wrong in this way. He had taken the trouble to study the market before he went out to buy his goods. He knew that taste and knowledge were to be bought just as easily as chairs and tables, and he went to the right shop. He employed a clever Scotchman, an artist in domestic furniture, to plan his house, and make drawings for the decoration and furniture of every room—and for six months he gave himself up to the task of furnishing.

Money was spent like water. Painters, decorators, cabinet-makers had a merry time of it. Royal Academicians were impressed into the service by large offers, and the final result of Mr. MacWalter's taste and Mr. Smithson's bullion was a palace in the style of the Italian Renaissance, frescoed ceilings, painted panels, a staircase of sculptured marble, as beautiful as a dream, a conservatory as exquisite as a jewel casket by

Benvenuto Cellini, a picture gallery which was the admiration of all London, and of the enlightened foreigner, and of the inquiring American. This was the house which Lesbia had been brought to see, and through which she walked with the calmly critical air of a person who had seen so many palaces that one more or less could make no difference.

In vain did Mr. Smithson peruse her countenance in the hope of seeing that she was impressed by the splendour of his surroundings, and by the power of the man who commanded such splendour. Lesbia was as cold as the Italian sculptor's Reading Girl in an alcove of Mr. Smithson's picture gallery: and the stockbroker felt very much as Aladdin might have done if the fair Badroulbadour had shown herself indifferent to the hall of the jewelled windows, in that magical palace which sprang into being in a single night.

Lesbia had been impressed by that story of poor Belle Trinder, and by Lady Kirkbank's broad assertion that half the young women in London were running after Mr. Smithson; and she had made up her mind to treat the man with supreme scorn. She did not want his houses or his yachts. Nothing could induce her to marry such a man, she told herself; but her vanity fed upon the idea of his subjugation, and her pride was gratified by the sense of her power over him.

The guests were few and choice. There was Mr. Meander, the poet, one of the leading lights in that new sect which prides itself upon the cultivation of abstract beauty, and occasionally touches the verge of concrete ugliness. There were a newspaper man—the editor of a fashionable journal—and a middle-aged man of letters, playwright, critic, humourist, a man whose society was in demand everywhere, and who said sharp things with the most supreme good-nature. The only ladies whose society Mr. Smithson had deemed worthy the occasion were a fashionable actress, with her younger sister, the younger a pretty copy of the elder, both dressed picturesquely in flowing cashmere gowns of faint sea-green, with old lace fichus, leghorn hats, and a general limpness and simplicity of style which suited their cast of feature and delicate colouring. Lesbia wondered to see how good an effect could be produced by a costume which could have cost so little. Mr. Nightshade, the famous tragedian, had been also asked to grace the feast, but the early hour made the invitation a mockery. It was not to be supposed that a man who went to bed at daybreak would get up again before the sun was in the zenith, for the sake of Mr. Smithson's society, or Mr. Smithson's Strasbourg pie, for the manufacture whereof a particular breed of geese were supposed to be set apart, like sacred birds in Egypt, while a particular vineyard in the Gironde was supposed to be devoted wholly and solely to the production of Mr. Smithson's claret. It was a cabinet wine, like those rare vintages of the Rhineland which are reserved exclusively for German princes.

Breakfast was served in Mr. Smithson's smallest dining-room—there were three apartments given up to feasting, beginning with a spacious banqueting-room for great dinners, and dwindling down to this snuggery, which held about a dozen comfortably, with ample room and verge enough for the attendants. The walls were upholstered in old gold silk, the curtains a tawny velvet of deeper tone, the cabinets and buffet of dark Italian walnut, inlaid with lapis-lazuli and amber, the fire-place a masterpiece of cabinet work, with high narrow shelves, and curious recesses holding priceless jars of Oriental enamel —the deep hearth filled up with arum lilies and azalias, like a font at Easter.

Lady Kirkbank, who pretended to adore genius, was affectionately effusive to Miss Fitzherbert, the popular actress, but she rather ignored the sister. Lesbia was less cordial, and was not enchanted at finding that Miss Fitzherbert shone and sparkled at the breakfast table by the gaiety of her spirits and the brightness of her conversation. There was something frank and joyous, almost to childishness, in the actress's manner, which was full of fascination; and Lesbia felt herself at a disadvantage almost for the first time since she had been in London.

The editor, the wit, the poet, the actress, had

a language of their own ; and Lesbia felt herself
out in the cold, unable to catch the ball as it
glanced past her, not quick enough to follow the
wit that evoked those ripples of silvery laughter
from the two fair-haired, pale-faced girls in sea-
green cashmere. She felt as an Englishman may
feel who has made himself master of academical
French, and who takes up one of Zola's novels,
or goes into artistic society, and finds that there
is another French, a complete and copious language,
of which he knows not a word.

Lesbia began to think that she had a great
deal to learn. She began to wonder even whether,
in the event of her having made rather too free
use of Lady Maulevrier's *carte blanche*, it might
not be well to make a new departure in the art
of dressing, and to wear untrimmed cashmere
gowns, and rags of limp lace.

After breakfast they all went to look at Mr.
Smithson's picture gallery. His pictures were, as
he had told Lesbia, chiefly of the French school,
and there may have been a remote period—say,
in the time of good Queen Charlotte—when such

pictures would hardly have been exhibited to young ladies. His pictures were Mr. Smithson's own unaided choice. Here the individual taste of the man stood revealed.

There were two or three Geromes: and in the place of honour at the end of the gallery there was a grand Delaroche, Anne Boleyn's last letter to the king, the hapless girl-queen sitting at a table in her cell in the Tower, a shaft of golden light from the narrow window streaming on the fair, disordered hair, the face bleached with un-utterable woe, a sublime image of despair and self-abandonment, all the rest of the cell in shadow.

The larger pictures were historical, classic, grand: but the smaller pictures—the lively little bits of colour dotted in here and there—were of that new school which Mr. Smithson affected. They were of that school which is called Im-pressionist, in which ballet dancers and jockeys, burlesque actresses, masked balls, and all the humours of the side-scenes are represented with the sublime audacity of an art which disdains finish, and relies on *chic, fougue, chien, flou,* the inspiration of the moment. Lesbia blushed as she looked at the ballet girls, the maskers in their scanty raiment, the *demi-mondaines* lolling out of their opera boxes, and half out of their gowns, with false smiles and frizzled hair. And then there came the works of that other school which lavishes the finish of a Meissonier on the most meretricious compositions. A woman in a velvet gown warming her dainty little feet on a gilded fender, in a boudoir all aglow with colour and lamp-light; a cavalier in satin raiment buckling his sword-belt before a Venetian mirror; a pair of lovers kissing in a sunlit corridor; a girl in a hansom cab; a milliner's shop; and so on, and so on.

Then came the classical subjects of the last new school. Weak imitations of Alma Tadema. Nero admiring his mother's corpse; Claudius interrupting Messalina's marriage with her lover Silius; Clodius disguised among the women of Cæsar's household; Pyrrha's grotto. Lady Kirk-bank expatiated upon all the pictures, and generally made unlucky guesses at the subjects of them. Classical literature was not her strong point.

Mr. Meander, the poet, discovered that all the beautiful heads were like Miss Fitzherbert. ‘ It is the same line,’ he exclaimed, ‘the line of lilies and flowing waters—the gracious ineffable upward returning ripple of the true *retroussé* nose, the divine *flou*, the loveliness which has lain dormant for centuries—nay, was at one period of debased art scorned and trampled under foot by the porcine herd, as akin to the pug and the turn-up, until discovered and enshrined on the altar of the Beautiful by the Boticelli Revivalists.’

Miss Fitzherbert simpered, and accepted these remarks as mere statements of obvious fact. She was accustomed to hear of Boticelli and the early Italian painters in connection with her own charms of face and figure.

Lesbia, whose faultless features were of the aquiline type, regarded the bard’s rhapsody as insufferable twaddle, and began to think Mr. Smithson almost a wit when he made fun of the bard.

Smithson was enchanted when she laughed at his jokelets, even although she did not scruple to tell him that she thought his favourite pictures detestable, and looked with the eye of indifference on a collection of jade that was worth a small fortune.

Mr. Meander fell into another rhapsody over those classic cups and shallow little bowls of absinthe-coloured jade.

'Here if you like, are colour and beauty, he murmured, caressing one of the little cups with the roseate tips of his supple fingers. 'These, dearest Smithson, are worth all the rest of your collection ; worth vanloads of your cloisonné enamels, your dragon-jars in blood-colour and blue. This cloudy indefinable substance, not crudely transparent nor yet distinctly opaque, a something which touches the boundary line of two worlds—the real and the ideal. And then the colour! Great heaven, can anything be lovelier than this shadowy tint which is neither yellow nor green; faint, faint as the dawn of newly-awakened day? I have seen just such a tinge in the sky going home from parties,' concluded the bard, smiling on the company, as they gathered round the Florentine table on which the jade specimens were set out Lady Kirkbank looking at the little cups and basins as if she thought they were going to do something, after all this fuss had been made about them. It seemed hardly credible that any reasonable being could have given thirty guineas for one of those bits of greenish-yellow clouded glass, unless the thing had some peculiar property of expansion or motion.

After this breakfast in Park Lane Lady Lesbia and her admirer met daily. He went to all her parties, he sat out waltzes with her, in conservatories, and on staircases; for Horace Smithson was much too shrewd a man to enter himself in the race for dancing men, handicapped by his forty years and his fourteen stone. He contrived to amuse Lesbia by his conversation, which was essentially mundane, depreciating people whom all the rest of the world admired, or pretended to admire, telling her of the secret springs by which the society she saw around was moved. He was judicious in his revelations of hidden evil, and careful to say nothing which should offend Lady Lesbia's womanly dignity; yet he contrived in a very short time to teach her that the world in which she lived was. an uttterly corrupt world, whose high priest was Satan; that all lofty aspirations and noble sentiments were out of place in society; and that the worst among the people she met were the people who laid any claim to being better than their neighbours.

'That's why I adore Lady Kirkbank,' he said confidentially. 'The dear soul never pretends to be any better than the rest of us. She gambles, and we all know she gambles; she pegs, and we all know she pegs; and she makes rather a boast of being up to her eyes in debt. No humbug about dear old Georgie Kirkbank.'

Lesbia had seen enough of her chaperon by this time to know that Mr. Smithson's description of the lady was correct, and, this being so, she supposed that the facts and traits of character which he told her about in other people were also true. She thus adopted the Smithsonian, or fashionable pessimist view of society in general, and resigned herself to the idea that the world was a very wicked world, as well as a very pleasant world, that the wickedest people were generally the pleasantest, and that it did not much matter.

The fact that Mr. Smithson was at Lesbia Haselden's feet was obvious to everybody.

Lesbia, who had at first treated him with supreme hauteur, had grown more civil as she began to understand the place he held in the world, and how much social influence goes along with unlimited wealth. She was civil, but she had quite made up her mind that nothing could ever induce her to become Horace Smithson's wife. That offer which had hung fire in the case of poor Belle Trinder, was not too long delayed on this occasion. Mr. Smithson called in Arlington Street about ten days after the breakfast in Park Lane, before luncheon, and before Lady Kirkbank had left her room. He brought tickets for a private matinée in Belgrave

Square, at which a new and wonderful Russian pianiste was to make a kind of semi-official *début* before an audience of critics and distinguished amateurs, and the very elect of the musical world. They were tickets which money could not buy, **and** were thus a meet offering for **Lady Lesbia**, and a plausible excuse for the early call.

Mr. Smithson succeeded in seeing Lesbia alone, and then and there, **with very** little circumlocution, **asked her to be his wife.**

Her social education had advanced with rapid strides since that summer day in the pine-wood, when John Hammond had wooed **her** with passionate wooing. Mr. Smithson **was** a much less **ardent** suitor, and made his offer with the air of **a man** who expects **to** be accepted.

Lesbia's beautiful head bent **a** little, like a lily on its stalk, and a faint, faint blush deepened the pale rose tint **of her** complexion. **Her** reply was courteous and conventional. She was flattered, she was grateful for Mr. Smithson's high opinion of her; but she was deeply grieved if anything in her manner had given him reason to think that he was more to her than a friend, an old friend of dear Lady Kirkbank's, whom she was naturally predisposed to like, as Lady Kirkbank's friend.

Horace Smithson turned pale as death, but if he was angry, he gave no utterance to his angry feelings. He only asked if Lady Lesbia's answer was final—and on being told that it was so, he dismissed the subject in the easiest manner, and with a gentlemanlike placidity which very much astonished the lady.

'You say that you regard me as your friend,' he said. '.Do not withdraw that privilege from me because I have asked for a higher place in your esteem. Forget all I have said this morning. Be assured I shall never offend you by repeating ·it.'

'You are more than good,' murmured Lesbia, who had expected a wild outbreak of despair or fury, rather than this friendly calm.

'I hope that you and Lady Kirkbank will go and hear Madame Metzikoff this afternoon,' pursued Mr. Smithson, returning to the subject of the *matinée*. 'The duchess's rooms are lovely: but no doubt you know them.'

Lesbia blushed, and confessed that the Duchess of Lostwithiel was one of those select few who were not on Lady Kirkbank's visiting list.

'There are people Lady Kirkbank cannot get on with,' she said. 'Perhaps she will hardly like to go to the duchess's, as she does not visit her.'

'Oh, but this affair counts for nothing. We go to hear Metzikoff, not to bow down to the duchess. All the people in town who care for music will be there, and you who play so divinely must enjoy fine professional playing.'

'I worship a really great player,' said Lesbia, 'and if I can drag Lady Kirkbank to the house of the enemy, we will be there.'

On this Mr. Smithson discreetly murmured '*au revoir*,' took up his hat and cane, and departed, without, in Sir George's parlance, having turned a hair.

'Refusal number one,' he said to himself, as he went downstairs, with his leisurely catlike pace, that velvet step by which he had gradually crept into society. 'We may have to go through refusal number two and number three; but she means to have me. She is a very clever girl for a countrybred one; and she knows that it is worth her while to be Lady Lesbia Smithson.'

This soliloquy may be taken to prove that Horace Smithson knew Lesbia Haselden better than she knew herself. She had refused him in all good faith; but even to-day, after he had left her, she fell into a day-dream in which Mr. Smithson's houses and yachts, drags and hunters, formed the shifting pictures in a dissolving view of society; and Lesbia wondered if there were any other young woman in London who would refuse such an offer as that which she had quietly rejected half an hour ago.

Lady Kirkbank surprised her while she was still absorbed in this dreamy review of the position. It is just possible that the fair Georgie may have had notice of Mr. Smithson's morning visit, and may have kept out of the way on purpose, for she was not a person of lazy habits, and was generally ready for her nine o'clock breakfast and her morning stroll in the park, however late she might have been out over-night.

'Mr. Smithson has been here, I understand,' said Lady Kirkbank, settling herself in an arm-chair by the open window, after she had kissed her *protégée*. 'Rilboche passed him on the stairs.'

'Rilboche is always passing people on the stairs,' answered Lesbia rather pettishly. 'I think she must spend her life on the landing, listening for arrivals and departures.'

'I had a kind of vague idea that Smithson would call to-day. He was so fussy about those tickets for the Metzikoff recital. I hate piano-forte recitals, and I detest that starched old duchess, but I suppose I shall have to take you there—or poor Smithson will be miserable,' said

Lady Kirkbank, watching Lesbia keenly over the top of her newspaper.

She expected Lesbia to confide in her, to announce herself blushingly as the betrothed of one of the richest commoners in England. But Lesbia sat gazing dreamily across the flowers in the balcony at the house over the way, and said never a word; so Lady Kirkbank's curiosity burst into speech.

'Well, my dear, has he proposed? There was something in his manner last night when he put on your wraps that made me think the crisis was near.'

'The crisis is come and is past, and Mr. Smithson and I are just as good friends as ever.'

'What!' screamed Lady Kirkbank. 'Do you mean to tell me that you have refused him?'

'Certainly. You know I never meant to do anything else. Did you think I was like Miss Trinder, bent upon marrying town and country houses, stables and diamonds?'

'I did not think you were a fool,' cried Lady Kirkbank, almost beside herself with vexation, for it had been borne in upon her, as the Methodists sometimes say, that if Mr. Smithson should prosper in his wooing it would be the better for her, Lady Kirkbank, who would have a claim upon his kindness ever after. 'What can be your motive in refusing one of the very best matches of the season—or of ever so many seasons? You think, perhaps, you will marry a duke, if you wait long enough for his Grace to appear: but the number of marrying dukes is rather small, Lady Lesbia, and I don't think any of those would care to marry Lord Maulevrier's granddaughter.'

Lesbia started to her feet, pale as ashes.

'Why do you fling my grandfather's name in my face—and with that diabolical sneer?' she exclaimed. 'When I have asked you about him you have always evaded my questions. Why should a man of the highest rank shrink from marrying Lord Maulevrier's granddaughter? My grandfather was a distinguished man—Governor of Madras. Such posts are not given to nobodies. How can you dare to speak as if it were a disgrace to me to belong to him?'

CHAPTER X.

' CLUBS, DIAMONDS, HEARTS, IN WILD DISORDER

SEEN.'

LADY KIRKBANK had considerable difficulty in smoothing Lesbia's ruffled plumage. She did all in her power to undo the effect of her rash words—declared that she had been carried away by temper—she had spoken she knew not what—words of no meaning. Of course Lesbia's grandfather had been a great man—Governor of Madras; altogether an important and celebrated person—and Lady Kirkbank had meant nothing, could have meant nothing to his disparagement.

' My dearest girl, I was beside myself, and talked sheer nonsense,' said Georgie. 'But you know really now, dearest, any woman of the world would be provoked at your foolish refusal of that dear good Smithson. Only think of that too lovely house in Park Lane, a palace in the style of the Italian Renaissance—such a house is in itself equivalent to a peerage—and there is no doubt Smithson will be offered a peerage before he is much older. I have heard it confidently asserted that when the present Ministry retires Smithson will be made a Peer. You have no idea what a useful man he is, or what henchman's service he has done the Ministry in financial matters. And then there is his villa at Deauville—you don't know Deauville—a positively perfect place, the villa, I mean, built by the Duke de Morny in the golden days of the Empire—and another at Cowes, and his place in Berkshire, a manor, my love, with a glorious old Tudor manor-house; and he has a *pied à terre* in Paris, in the Faubourg, a ground-floor furnished in the Pompeian style, half-a-dozen rooms opening one out of the other, and surrounding a small

garden, with a fountain in the middle. Some
of the greatest people in Paris occupy the
upper part of the house, and their rooms of
course are splendid ; but Smithson's ground-floor
is the gem of the Faubourg. However, I
suppose there is no use in talking any more ;
and there is the gong for luncheon.'

Lesbia was in no humour for luncheon.

'I would rather have a cup of tea in my
own room,' she said. 'This Smithson business
has given me an abominable headache.'

'But you will go to hear Metzikoff ? '

'No, thanks. You detest the Duchess of
Lostwithiel, and you don't care for pianoforte
recitals. Why should I drag you there ? '

'But, my dearest Lesbia, I am not such a
selfish wretch as to keep you at home, when I
know you are passionately fond of good music.
Forget all about your headache, and let me
see how that lovely little Catherine of Aragon
bonnet suits you. I'm so glad I happened to
see it in Seraphine's hands yesterday, just as
she was going to send t to Lady Fonvielle,

who gives herself such intolerable airs on the strength of a pretty face, and always wants to get the *primeurs* in bonnets and things.'

'Another new bonnet!' replied Lesbia. 'What an infinity of things I seem to be having from Seraphine. I'm afraid I must owe her a good deal of money.'

This was a vague way of speaking about actual facts. Lady Lesbia might have spoken with more certainty. Her wardrobes and old-fashioned hanging closets and chests of drawers in Arlington Street were crammed to overflowing with finery; and then there were all the things that she had grown tired of, or had thought unbecoming, and had given away to Kibble, her own maid, or to Rilboche, who had in a great measure superseded Kibble on all important occasions; for how could a Westmoreland girl know how to dress a young lady for London balls and drawing-rooms?

'If you had only accepted Mr. Smithson it would not matter how much money you owed people,' said Lady Kirkbank. 'You had better come down to lunch. A glass of Heidseck will bring you up to 'concert pitch.'

Champagne was Lady Kirkbank's idea of a universal panacea ; and she had gradually succeeded in teaching Lesbia to believe in the sovereign power of Heidseck as a restorative for shattered nerves. At Fellside Lesbia had drunk only water ; but then at Fellside she had never known that feeling of exhaustion and prostration which follows days and nights spent in society, the wear and tear of a mind for ever on the alert, and brilliant spirits which are more often forced than real. For her chief stimulant Lesbia had recourse to the teapot : but there were occasions when she found that something more than tea was needed to maintain that indispensable vivacity of manner which Lady Kirkbank called concert pitch.

To-day she allowed herself to be persuaded. She went down to luncheon, and took a couple of glasses of dry champagne with her cutlet, and, thus restored, was equal to putting on the new bonnet, which was so becoming that her spirits revived as she contemplated the effect in her glass. So

Lady Kirkbank carried her off to the musical matinée, beaming and radiant, having forgotten all about that dark hint of evil glancing at the name of her long dead grandfather.

The duchess was not on view when Lady Kirkbank and her *protégée* arrived, and a good many people belonging to Georgie's own particular set were scattered like flowers among those real music-lovers who had come solely to hear the new pianiste. The music-lovers were mostly dowdy in their attire, and seemed a race apart. Among them were several young women of the Blessed Damozel school, who wore flowing garments of sap-green or ochre, or puffed raiment of Venetian red, and among whom the cart-wheel hat, the Elizabethan sleeve, and the Toby frill were conspicuous.

There were very few men except the musical critics in this select assemblage, and Lesbia began to think that it was going to be very dreary. She had lived in such an atmosphere of masculine adulation while under Lady Kirkbank's wing that it was a new thing to find herself in a room where there were none to love and very few to praise her. She felt out in the cold, as it were. Those ungloved critics, with their shabby coats and dubious shirts, snuffy, smoky, everything they ought not to be, seemed to her a race of barbarians.

Finding herself thus cold and lonely in the midst of the duchess's splendour of peacock-blue velvet and peacock-feather decoration, Lesbia was almost glad when in the middle of Madame Metzikoff's opening gondolied—airy, fairy music, executed with surpassing delicacy—Mr. Smithson crept gently into the *fauteuil* just behind hers, and leant over the back of the chair to whisper an inquiry as to her opinion of the pianist's style.

'She is exquisite,' Lesbia murmured softly, but the whispered question and the murmured answer, low as they were, provoked indignant looks from a brace of damsels in Venetian red, who shook their Toby frills with an outraged air.

Lesbia felt that Mr. Smithson's presence was hardly correct. It would have been 'better form' if he had stayed away; and yet she was glad to have him here. At the worst he was some one—

nay, according to Lady Kirkbank, he was the only one amongst all her admirers whose offer was worth having. All Lesbia's other conquests had counted as barren honour; but if she could have brought herself to accept Mr. Smithson she would have secured the very best match of the season.

To marry a plain Mr. Smithson—a man who had made his money in iron—in cochineal—on the Stock Exchange—had seemed to her absolute degradation, the surrender of all her lofty hopes, her golden dreams. But Lady Kirkbank had put the question in a new light when she said that Smithson would be offered a peerage. Smithson the peer would be altogether a different person from Smithson the commoner.

But was Lady Kirkbank sure of her facts, or truthful in her statement? Lesbia's experience of her chaperon's somewhat loose notions of truth and exactitude made her doubtful upon this point.

Be this as it might she was inclined to be civil to Smithson, albeit she was inwardly surprised and offended at his taking her refusal so calmly.

'You see that I am determined not to lose the

privilege of your society, because I have been foolish!' he said presently, in the pause after the first part of the recital. 'I hope you will consider me as much your friend to-day as I was yesterday.'

'Quite as much,' she answered sweetly, and then they talked of Raff, and Rubenstein, and Henselt, and all the composers about whom it is the correct thing to discourse nowadays.

Before they left Belgrave Square Lady Kirk-bank had offered Mr. Smithson Sir George's place in her box at the Gaiety that evening, and had invited him to supper in Arlington Street afterwards.

It was Sarah Bernhardt's first season in London—the never-to-be-forgotten season of the Comédie Française.

'I should love of all things to be there,' said Mr. Smithson, meekly. He had a couple of stalls in the third row for the whole of the season. 'But how can I be sure that I shall not be turning Sir George out of doors?'

'Sir George can never sit out a serious play. He only cares for Chaumont or Judic. The Demi-monde is much too prosy for him.'

'The Demi-monde is one of the finest plays in the French language,' said Smithson. 'You know it, of course, Lady Lesbia?'

'Alas! no. At Fellside I was not allowed to read French plays or novels: or only a novel now and then, which my grandmother selected for me.'

'And now you read everything, I suppose,— including Zola?'

'The books are lying about, and I dip into them sometimes while I am having my hair brushed,' answered Lesbia, lightly.

'I believe that is the only time ladies devote to literature during the season,' said Mr. Smithson. 'Well, I envy you the delight of seeing the Demi-monde without knowing what it is all about beforehand.'

'I daresay there are a good many people who would not take their girls to see a play by Dumas,' said Lady Kirkbank, 'but I make a point of letting *my* girls see everything. It widens their minds and awakens their intelli-gence'

'And does **away with a** good many silly prejudices,' replied Mr. Smithson.

Lady Kirkbank **and** Lesbia **were** due **at a** Kensington garden-party after the recital, and from the garden-party, for which an hour sufficed, they **went** to show themselves **in** the Park, then back to **Arlington Street** to dress for the play. Then **a** hurried dinner, **and** they were in their places **at the** theatre **in** time for **the** rising of the curtain.

'If it were an English play we would not care for being **punctual,'** said Lady Kirkbank; 'but **I** should hate to lose **a** word . of Dumas. In his **plays** every speech tells.'

There were Royalties present, and the house was good; but not so full **as it** had been on some other nights, for the English public had been told **that Sarah** Bernhardt **was** the person to admire, and had been flocking sheep-like after that golden-haired enchantress, whereby many **of** these sheep—fighting greedily for Sarah's nights, and ignoring all other talent—lost some of the finest acting on the French stage, notably that of Croizette, Delaunay and Febvre, in this very

Demi-monde. Lesbia, who, in spite of her affectations, was still fresh enough to be charmed with fine acting and a powerful play, was enthralled by the stage, so wrapt in the scene that she was quite unaware of her brother's presence in a stall just below Lady Kirkbank's box. He too had a stall at the Gaiety. He had come in very late, when the play was half over. Lesbia was surprised when he presented himself at the door of the box, after the fourth act.

Maulevrier and his sister had met very seldom since the young lady's *début*. The young Earl did not go to many parties, and the society he cultivated was chiefly masculine; and as he neither played polo nor shot pigeons his masculine pursuits did not bring him in his sister's way. Lady Kirkbank had asked him to her house with that wide and general invitation which is so easily evaded. He had promised to go, and he had not gone. And thus Lesbia and he had pursued their several ways, only crossing each other's paths now and then at a race meeting or in a theatre.]

'How d'ye do, Lady Kirkbank?—how d'ye do,

Lesbia? Just caught sight of you from below as the curtain was going down,' said Maulevrier, shaking hands with the ladies and saluting Mr. Smithson with a somewhat supercilious nod. ' Rather surprised to see you and Lesbia here to-night, Lady Kirkbank. Isn't the Demi-monde rather strong meat for babes, eh? Not *exactly* the play one would take a young lady to see.'

'Why should a young lady be forbidden to see a fine play, because there are some hard and bitter truths told in it?' asked Lady Kirkbank. 'Lesbia sees Madame d'Ange and all her sisterhood in the Park and about London every day of her life. Why should not she see them on the stage, and hear their history, and understand how cruel their fate is, and learn to pity them, if she can? I really think this play is a lesson in Christian charity; and I should like to see that Oliver man strangled, though Delaunay plays the part divinely. What a voice! What a manner How polished! How perfect! And they tell me he is going to leave the stage in a year or two. What will the world do without him?'

Maulevrier did not attempt to suggest a solution of this difficulty. He was watching Mr. Smithson as he leant against the back of Lesbia's chair and talked to her. The two seemed very familiar, laughingly discussing the play and the actors. Smithson knew, or pretended to know, all about the latter. He told Lesbia who made Croizette's gowns—the upholsterer who furnished that lovely house of hers in the Bois—the sums paid for her horses, her pictures, her diamonds. It seemed to Lesbia, when she had heard all, that Croizette was a much-to-be-envied person.

Mr. Smithson had unpublished *bon-mots* of Dumas at his finger ends; he knew Daudet, and Sarcey, and Sardou, and seemed to be thoroughly at home in Parisian artistic society. Lesbia began to think that he would hardly be so despicable a person as she had at first supposed. No wonder he and his wealth had turned poor Belle Trinder's head. How could a rural vicar's daughter, accustomed to poverty, help being dazzled by such magnificence?

Maulevrier stayed in the box only a short time, and refused Lady Kirkbank's invitation to supper. She did not urge the point, as she had surprised one or two very unfriendly glances at Mr. Smithson in Maulevrier's honest eyes. She did not want an antagonistic brother to interfere with her plans. She had made up her mind to 'run' Lesbia according to her own ideas, and any counter influence might be fatal. So when Maulevrier said he was due at the Marlborough after the play she let him go.

'I might as well be at Fellside and you in London, for anything I see of you,' said Lesbia.

'You are up to your eyes in engagements, and I don't suppose you want to see any more of me,' Maulevrier answered, bluntly. 'But I'll call to-morrow morning, if I am likely to find you at home. I've some news for you.'

'Then I'll stay at home on purpose to see you. News is always delightful. Is it good news, by-the-bye?'

'Very good; at least, I think so.'

'What is it about?'

'Oh, that's a long story, and the curtain is just going up. The news is about Mary.'

'About Mary!' exclaimed Lesbia, elevating her eyebrows. 'What news can there possibly be about Mary?'

'Such news as there generally is about every nice jolly girl, at least once in her life.'

'You don't mean that she is engaged—to a curate?'

'No, not to a curate. There goes the curtain. "I'll see you later," as the Yankee President used to say when people bothered him, and he didn't like to say no.'

Engaged! Mary. engaged! The idea of such an altogether unexpected event distracted Lesbia's mind all through the last act of the Demi-monde. She hardly knew what the actors were talking about. Mary, her younger sister! Mary, a good looking girl enough, but by no means a beauty, and with manners utterly unformed. That Mary should be engaged to be married, while she, Lesbia, was still free, seemed an obvious absurdity.

And yet the fact was, on reflection, easily to be accounted for. These unattractive girls are generally the first to bind themselves with the vows of betrothal. Lady Kirkbank had told her of many such cases. The poor creatures know that their chances will be few, and therefore gratefully welcome the first wooer.

'But who can the man be?' thought Lesbia. 'Mary has been kept as secluded as a cloistered nun. There are so few families we have ever been allowed to mix with. The man must be a curate, who has taken advantage of grand-mother's illness to force his way into the family circle at Fellside—and who has made love to Mary in some of her lonely rambles over the hills, I daresay. It is really very wrong to allow a girl to roam about in that way.'

Sir George and a couple of his horsey friends were waiting for supper when Lady Kirkbank and her party arrived in Arlington Street. The dining-room looked a picture of comfort. The oval table, the low lamps, the clusters of candles under coloured shades, the great Oriental bowl of wild flowers—eglantine, honeysuckle, foxglove, all the sweet hedge flowers of midsummer, made a central mass of colour and brightness against the subdued and even sombre tones of walls and curtains. The room was old, the furniture old. Nothing had been altered since the time of Sir George's great grandfather; and the whirligig of time had just now made the old things precious. Yes, those chairs and tables and sideboards and bookcases and wine-coolers against which Georgie's soul had revolted in the early years of her wedded life were now things of beauty, and Georgie's friends envied her the possession of indisputable Chippendale furniture.

Mr. Mostyn, a distinguished owner of race-horses, with his pretty wife, made up the party. The gentleman, was full of his entries for Liverpool · and Chester, and discoursed mysteriously with Sir George and the horsey bachelors all supper time. The lady had lately taken up science as a new form of excitement, not incompatible with frocks, bonnets, Hurlingham, the Ranelagh, and Sandown. She raved about Huxley and Tyndall, and was perpetually coming down upon her friends with awful facts about the sun, and startling propositions about latent heat, or spontaneous generation. She knew all about gases, and would hardly accept a glass of water without explaining what it was made of. Drawn by Mr. Smithson for Lesbia's amusement, the scientific matron was undoubtedly 'good fun.' The racing men were full of talk. Lesbia and Lady Kirkbank raved about the play they had just been seeing, and praised Delaunay with an enthusiasm which was calculated to make the rest of mankind burst with envy.

'Do you know you are making me positively wretched by your talk about that man?' said Colonel Delville, one of Sir George's racing friends, and an ancient adorer of the fair Georgie's. 'No, I tell you there was never anything offered higher than five to four on the mare,' interjectionally, to Sir George. 'There was a day when I thought I was your idea of an attractive man. Yes, George, a clear case of roping,' again interjectionally. 'And now to hear you raving about this play-acting fellow—it is too humiliating.'

Lady Kirkbank simpered, and then sighed.

'We are getting old together,' she murmured.

'I have come to an age when one can only admire the charm of manner in the abstract—the Beautiful for the sake of the Beautiful. I think if I were lying in my grave, the music of Delaunay's voice would thrill me, under six feet of London clay. Will no one take any more wine? No. Then we may as well go into the next room and begin our little Nap.'

The adjoining room was Sir George's snuggery; and it was here that the cosy little round games after supper were always played. Sir George was not a studious person. He never read, and he never wrote, except an occasional cheque on account, for an importunate tradesman. His correspondence was conducted by the telegraph or the telephone; and the room, therefore, was absorbed neither by books nor writing desks. It was furnished solely with a view to comfort. There was a round table in the centre, under a large moderator lamp which gave an exceptionally brilliant light. A divan covered with dark brown velvet occupied three sides of the room. A few choice pieces of old blue Oriental ware in the

corners enlivened the dark brown walls. Three
or four easy chairs stood about near the broad,
old-fashioned fireplace, which had been improved
with a modern-antique brass grate and a blue and
white tiled hearth.

'There isn't a room in my house that looks half
as comfortable as this den of yours, George,' said
Mr. Smithson, as he seated himself by Lesbia's
side at the card table.

They had agreed to be partners. 'Partners at
cards, even if we are not to be partners for life,'
Smithson had whispered, tenderly ; and Lesbia's
only reply had been a modest lowering of lovely
eyelids, and a faint, faint blush. Lesbia's blushes
were growing fainter every day.

'That is because everything in your house is
so confoundedly handsome and expensive,' retorted
Sir George, who did not very much care about
being called George, *tout court*, by a person of
Mr. Smithson's obscure antecedents, but who had
to endure the familiarity for reasons known only
to himself and Mr. Smithson. 'No man can expect
to be comfortable in a house in which every room

has cost a small fortune. My wife re-arranged this den half-a-dozen years ago when we took to sittin' here of an evenin'. She picked up the chairs and the blue pots at Bonham's, had everythin' covered with brown velvet—nice subdued tone, suit old people—hung up that yaller curtain, just for a bit of colour, and here we are.'

'It's the cosiest room in town,' said Colonel Delville, whereupon Mrs. Mostyn, while counters were being distributed, explained to the company on scientific principles *why* the room was comfortable, expatiating upon the effect of yellow and brown upon the retina, and adding some curious facts relating to the optic machinery of water-fleas, as lately discovered by a great naturalist.

Unfortunately for science, the game had now begun, and the players were curiously indifferent as to the visual organs of water-fleas.

The game went on merrily till the pearly lights of dawn began to creep through the chinks of Lady Kirkbank's yellow curtain. Everybody seemed gay, yet everybody could not be winning. Fortune had not smiled upon Lesbia's cards, or on those of her partner. The Smithson and Haselden firm had come to grief. Lesbia's little ivory purse had been emptied of its three or four half-sovereigns, and Mr. Smithson had been capitalising a losing concern for the last two hours. And the play had been fast and furious, although nominally for small stakes.

'I am afraid to think of how much I must owe you,' said Lesbia, when Mr. Smithson bade her good night.

'Oh, nothing worth speaking of—sixteen or seventeen pounds, at most.'

Lesbia felt cold and creepy, and hardly knew whether it was the chill of new-born day, or the sense of owing money to Horace Smithson. Those three or four half-sovereigns to-night were the end of her last remittance from Lady Maulevrier. She had had a great many remittances from that generous grandmother; and the money had all gone, somehow. It was gone, and yet she had paid for hardly anything. She had accounts with all Lady Kirkbank's tradesmen. The money had melted away—it had oozed out of her pockets—

at cards, on the race-course, in reckless gifts to
servants and people, at fancy fairs, for trifles
bought here and there by the way-side, as it
were, for the sake of buying. If she had been
suddenly asked for an account of her steward-
ship she could not have told what she had done
with half of the money. And now she must
ask for twenty pounds more, and immediately,
to pay Mr. Smithson.

She went up to her room in the clear early
light, and stood like a statue, with fixed thoughtful eyes, while Kibble took off her finery, the
pretty pale yellow gown which set off her dark
brown hair, her violet eyes. For the first time
in her life she felt the keen pang of anxiety
about money matters—the necessity to think of
ways and means. She had no idea how much
money she had received from her grandmother
since she had begun her career in Scotland last
autumn. The cheques had been sent her as she
asked for them; sometimes even before she
asked for them; and she had kept no account.
She thought her grandmother was so rich that

expenditure could not matter. She supposed that she was drawing upon an inexhaustible supply. And now Lady Kirkbank had told her that Lady Maulevrier was not rich, as the world reckons nowadays. The savings of a dowager countess even in forty years of seclusion could be but a small fund to draw upon for the expenses of life at high pressure.

'The sums people spend nowadays are positively appalling,' said Lady Kirkbank. 'A man with five or six thousand a year is an absolute pauper. I'm sure our existence is only genteel beggary, and yet we spend over ten thousand.'

Enlightened thus by the lips of the worldly-wise, Lesbia thought ruefully of the bills which her grandmother would have to pay for her at the end of the season, bills of the amount whereof she could not even make an approximate guess. Seraphine's charges had never been discussed in her hearing—but Lady Kirkbank had admitted that the creature was dear.

CHAPTER XI.

'SWIFT SUBTLE POST, CARRIER OF GRISLY CARE.'

MAULEVRIER called in Arlington Street before twelve o'clock next day, and found Lesbia just returning from her early ride, looking as fresh and fair as if there had been no such thing as Nap or late hours in the story of her life. She was reposing in a large easy chair by the open window, in habit and hat, just as she had come from the Row, where she had been laughing and chatting with Mr. Smithson, who jogged demurely by her side on his short-legged hunter, dropping out envenomed little jokes about the passers by. People who saw him riding by her side upon this particular morning fancied there was something more than usual in the gentleman's manner, and made up their minds that Lady Lesbia Haselden was to be mistress of the fine house in

Park Lane. Mr. Smithson had fluttered and fluttered for the last five seasons ; but this time the flutterer was caught.

In her newly-awakened anxiety about money matters, Lesbia had forgotten Mary's engagement ; but the sight of Maulevrier recalled the fact.

'Come over here and sit down,' she said, 'and tell me this nonsense about Mary. I am expiring with curiosity. The thing is too absurd.'

'Why absurd?' asked Maulevrier, sitting where she bade him, and studiously perusing the name in his hat, as if it were a revelation.

'Oh, for a thousand reasons,' answered Lesbia, switching the flowers in the balcony with her light little whip. 'First and foremost it is absurd to think of any one so buried alive as poor Mary is finding an admirer ; and secondly—well—I don't want to be rude to my own sister—but Mary is not particularly attractive.'

'Mary is the dearest girl in the world.'

'Very likely. I only said that she is not particularly attractive.'

'And do you think there is no attraction in

goodness, in freshness and innocence, candour, generosity —— ? '

'I don't know. But I think that if Mary's nose had been a thought longer, and if she had kept her skin free from freckles she would have been almost pretty.'

'Do you really? Luckily for Mary the man who is going to marry her thinks her lovely.'

'I suppose he likes freckles. I once heard a man say he did. He said they were so original —so much character about them. And, pray, who is the man?'

'Your old adorer, and my dear friend, John Hammond.'

Lesbia turned as pale as death—pale with rage and mortification. It was not jealousy, this pang which rent her shallow soul. She had ceased to care for John Hammond. The whirlpool of society had spun that first fancy out of her giddy brain. But that a man who had loved the highest, who had worshipped her, the peerless, the beautiful, should calmly transfer his affections to her younger sister, was to the last degree exasperating.

'Your friend Mr. Hammond must be a fickle fool,' she exclaimed, 'who does not know his own mind from day to day.'

'Oh, but it was more than a day after you rejected him that he engaged himself to Molly. It was all my doing, and I am proud of my work. I took the poor fellow back to Fellside last March, bruised and broken by your cruel treatment, heartsore and depressed. I gave him over to Molly, and Molly cured him. Unconsciously, innocently, she won that noble heart. Ah, Lesbia, you don't know what a heart it is which you so nearly broke.'

'Girls in our rank of life can't afford to marry noble hearts,' said Lesbia, scornfully. 'Do you mean to tell me that Lady Maulevrier consented to the engagement?'

'She cut up rather rough at first; but Molly held her own like a young lioness—and the grandmother gave way. You see she has a fixed idea that Molly is a very second-rate sort of person compared with you, and that a husband who was not nearly good enough for you might pass muster for Molly; and so she gave way, and there isn't a happier young woman in the three kingdoms than Mary Haselden.'

'What are they to live upon?' asked Lesbia, with an incredulous air.

'Mary will have her five hundred a year. And Hammond is a very clever fellow. You may be sure he will make his mark in the world.'

'And how are they to live while he is making his mark? Five hundred a year won't do more than pay for Mary's frocks, if she goes into society.'

'Perhaps they will live without society.'

'In some horrid little hovel in one of those narrow streets off Ecclestone Square,' suggested Lesbia, shudderingly. 'It is too dreadful to think of—a young woman dooming herself to life-long penury, just because she is so foolish as to fall in love.'

'Your days for falling in love are over, I suppose, Lesbia?' said Maulevrier, contemplating his sister with keen scrutiny.

The beautiful face, so perfect in line and colour, curiously recalled that other face at Fellside; the dowager's face, with its look of marble coldness, and the half-expressed pain under that outward calm. Here was the face of one who had not yet known pain or passion. Here was the cold perfection of beauty with unawakened heart.

'I don't know; I am too busy to think of such things.'

'You have done with love; and you have begun to think of marriage, of establishing yourself properly. People tell me you are going to marry Mr. Smithson.'

'People tell you more about me than I know about myself.'

'Come now, Lesbia, I have a right to know the truth upon this point. Your brother—your only brother—should be the first person to be told.'

'When I am engaged, I have no doubt you will be the first person, or the second person,' answered Lesbia, lightly. 'Lady Kirkbank, living on the premises, is likely to be the first.'

'Then you are not engaged to Smithson?'

'Didn't I tell you so just now? Mr. Smithson did me the honour to make me an offer yesterday, at about this hour; and I did myself the honour to reject him.'

'And yet you were whispering together in the box last night, and you were riding in the Row with him this morning. I just met a fellow who saw you together. Do you think it is right, Lesbia, to play fast and loose with the man—to encourage him, if you don't mean to marry him?'

'How can you accuse me of encouraging a person whom I flatly refused yesterday morning? If Mr. Smithson likes my society as a friend, must I needs deny him my friendship, ask Lady Kirkbank to shut her door against him? Mr. Smithson is very pleasant as an acquaintance; and although I don't want to marry him, there's no reason I should snub him.'

'Smithson is not a man to be trifled with. You will find yourself entangled in a web which you won't easily break through.'

'I am not afraid of webs. By-the-bye, is it

true that Mr. Smithson is likely to get a peerage ? '

' I have heard people say as much. Smithson has spent no end of money on electioneering, and is a power in the House, though he very rarely speaks. His Berkshire estate gives him a good deal of influence in that county; at the last general election he subscribed twenty thou to the Conservative cause ; for, like most men who have risen from nothing, your friend Smithson is a fine old Tory. He was specially elected at the Carlton six years ago, and has made himself uncommonly useful to his party. He is supposed to be great on financial questions, and comes out tremendously on colonial railways or drainage schemes, about which the House in general is in profound igno- rance. On those occasions Smithson scores high. A man with immense wealth has always chances. No doubt, if you were to marry him, the peerage would be easily managed. Smithson's money, backed by the Maulevrier influence, would go a long way. My grandmother would move heaven and earth in a case of that kind. You had better take pity on Smithson.'

Lesbia laughed. That idea of a possible peerage elevated Smithson in her eyes. She knew nothing of his political career, as she lived in a set which ignored politics altogether. Mr. Smithson had never talked to her of his parliamentary duties; and it was a new thing for her to hear that he had some kind of influence in public affairs.

'Suppose I were inclined to accept him, would you like him as a brother-in-law?' she asked lightly. 'I thought from your manner last night that you rather disliked him.'

'I don't quite like him or any of his breed, the newly rich, who go about in society swelling with the sense of their own importance, perspiring gold, as it were. And one has always a faint suspicion of men who have got rich very quickly, an idea that there must be some kind of juggling. Not in the case of a great contractor, perhaps, who can point to a viaduct and docks and railways, and say, "I built that, and that, and that. These are the sources of my wealth." But a man who gets enormously rich by mere ciphering! Where can his money come from, except out of other people's pockets? I know nothing against your Mr. Smithson, but I always suspect that class of men,' concluded Maulevrier, shaking his head significantly.

Lesbia **was not** much influenced by her brother's notions. She had never been taught to think him an oracle. On the contrary, she **had been** told that his life hitherto had been all foolishness.

'When are Mary and Mr. Hammond to be married?' she asked.

'Grandmother **says they must wait** a year. Mary is much too young—and **so on,** and so forth. **But I** see no reason for waiting.'

'Surely there **are** reasons—financial reasons. Mr. Hammond cannot be in a position to begin housekeeping.'

'Oh, they will risk all that. Molly is a **daring** girl. He proposed to her on the top of Helvellyn, in a storm of wind and rain.'

'And she never wrote **me a** word about it. How very unsisterly!'

'She is as wild as **a** hawk, **and I** daresay she **was too shy to tell you anything about it.'**

' Pray when did it all occur ? '

' Just before I came to London.'

' Two months ago. How absurd for me to be in ignorance all this time! Well, I hope Mary will be sensible, and not marry till Mr. Hammond is able to give her a decent home. It would be so dreadful to have a sister muddling in poverty, and clamouring for one's cast-off gowns.'

Maulevrier laughed at this gloomy suggestion.

' It is not easy to foretell the future,' he said, ' but I think I may venture to promise that Molly will never wear your cast-off gowns.'

' Oh, you think she would be too proud. You don't know, perhaps, how poverty—genteel poverty —lowers one's pride. I have heard stories from Lady Kirkbank that would make your hair stand on end. I am beginning to know the world.'

' I am glad of that. If you are to live in the world it is better that you should know what it is made of. But if I had a voice or a choice in the matter I had rather my sisters stayed at Grasmere, and remained ignorant of the world and all its ways.'

'While you enjoy your life in London. That is just like the selfishness of a man. Under the pretence of keeping his sisters or his wife secure from all possible contact with evil, he buries them alive in a country house, while he has all the wickedness for his own share in London. Oh, I am beginning to understand the creatures.'

'I am afraid you are beginning to be wise. Remember that knowledge of evil was the prelude to the Fall. Well, good-bye.'

'Won't you stay to lunch?'

'No, thanks, I never lunch—frightful waste of time. I shall drop in at the *Haute Gomme* and take a cup of tea later on.'

The *Haute Gomme* was a new club in Piccadilly, which Maulevrier and some of his friends affected.

Lesbia went towards the drawing-room door with her brother, and just as he reached the door she laid her hand caressingly upon his shoulder. He turned and stared at her, somewhat surprised, for he and she had never been given to demonstrations of affection.

'Maulevrier, I want you to do me a favour,' she said, in a low voice, blushing a little, for the thing she was going to ask was a new thing for her to ask, and she had a deep sense of shame in making her demand. 'I—I lost money at Nap last night. Only seventeen pounds. Mr. Smithson and I were partners, and he paid my losses. I want to pay him immediately, and——'

'And you are too hard up to do it. I'll write you a cheque this instant,' said Maulevrier, good-naturedly; but while he was writing the cheque he took occasion to remonstrate with Lesbia on the foolishness of card playing.

'I am obliged to do as Lady Kirkbank does,' she answered feebly. 'If I were to refuse to play it would be a kind of reproach to her.'

'I don't think that would kill Lady Kirkbank,' replied Maulevrier, with a touch of scorn. 'She has had to endure a good many implied reproaches in her day, and they don't seem to have hurt her very much. I wish to heaven my grandmother had chosen any one else in London for your chaperon.'

'I'm afraid Lady Kirkbank's is rather a rowdy set,' answered Lesbia, coolly; 'and I sometimes feel as if I had thrown myself away. We go almost everywhere—at least, there are only just a few houses to which we are not asked. But those few make all the difference. It is so humiliating to feel that one is not in quite the best society. However, Lady Kirkbank is a dear, good old thing, and I am not going to grumble about her.'

'I've made the cheque for five-and-twenty. You can cash it at your milliner's,' said Maulevrier. 'I should not like Smithson to know that you had been obliged to ask me for the money.'

'*Apropos* to Mr. Smithson, do you know if he is in quite the best society?' asked Lesbia.

'I don't know what you mean by quite the best. A man of Smithson's wealth can generally poke his nose in anywhere, if he knows how to behave himself. But of course there are people with whom money and fine houses have no weight. The Conservatives are all civil to Smithson because he comes down handsomely at General Elections, and is useful to them in other ways. I believe that Smithson's wife, if she were a thoroughbred one, could go into any society she liked, and make her house one of the most popular in London. Perhaps that is what you really wanted to ask.'

'No, it wasn't,' answered Lesbia, carelessly; 'I was only talking for the sake of talking. A thousand thanks for the cheque, you best of brothers.'

'It is not worth talking about; but, Lesbia, don't play cards any more. Believe me, it is not good form.'

'Well, I'll try to keep out of it in future. It is horrid to see one's sovereigns melting away; but there's a delightful excitement in winning.'

'No doubt,' answered Maulevrier, with a remorseful sigh.

He spoke as a reformed plunger, and with many a bitter experience of the racecourse and the card-room. Even now, though he had steadied himself wonderfully, he could not get on without a little mild gambling—half-crown pool, whist with half-guinea points—but when he conde-scended to such small stakes he felt that he had settled down into a respectable middle-aged player, and had a right to rebuke the follies of youth.

Lesbia flew to the piano and sang one of her little German ballads directly Maulevrier was gone. She felt as if a burden had been lifted from her soul, now that she was able to pay Mr. Smithson without waiting to ask Lady Maulevrier for the money. And as she sang she meditated upon Maulevrier's remarks about Smithson. He knew nothing to the man's discredit, except that he had grown rich in a short space of time. Surely no man ought to be blamed for that. And he thought that Mr. Smithson's wife might make her house the most popular in London. Lesbia, in her mind's eye, beheld an imaginary Lady Lesbia Smithson giving dances in that magnificent mansion, entertaining Royal personages. And the doorways would be festooned with roses, as she had seen them the other night at a ball in Grosvenor Square; but the house in Grosvenor Square was a hovel compared with the Smithsonian Palace.

Lesbia was beginning to be a little tired of Lady Kirkbank and her surroundings. Life taken *prestissimo* is apt to pall. Lesbia sighed as she finished her little song. She was beginning to look upon her existence as a problem which had been given to her to solve, and the solution just at present was all dark.

As she rose from the piano a footman came in with two letters on a salver—bulky letters, such packages as Lesbia had never seen before. She wondered what they could be. She opened the thickest envelope first. It was Seraphine's bill—such a bill, page after page on creamy Bath post, written in an elegant Italian hand by one of Seraphine's young women.

Lesbia looked at it aghast with horror. The total at the foot of the first page was appalling, ever so much more than she could have supposed the whole amount of her indebtedness; but the total went on increasing at the foot of every page, until at sight of the final figures Lesbia gave a wild shriek, like a wretched creature who has received a telegram announcing bitterest loss.

The final total was twelve hundred and ninety-three pounds seventeen and sixpence !

Thirteen hundred pounds for clothes in eight weeks!

No, the thing was a cheat, a mistake. They had sent her somebody else's bill. She had not had half these things.

She read the first page, her heart beating violently as she pored over the figures, her eyes dim and clouded with the trouble of her brain.

Yes, there was her court dress. The description was too minute to be mistaken ; and the court dress, with feathers, and shoes, and gloves, and fan, came to a hundred and thirty pounds. Then followed innumerable items. The very simplest of her gowns cost five-and-twenty pounds —frocks about which Seraphine had talked so carelessly, as if two or three more or less could make no difference. Bonnets and hats, at five or seven guineas apiece, swelled the account. Parasols and fans were of fabulous price, as it seemed to Lesbia ; and the shoes and stockings to match her various gowns occurred again and again between the more important items, like the refrain of an old ballad. All the useless and unnecessary things which she had ordered, because she thought them pretty or because she was told they were fashionable, rose up against her in the figures of the bill like the record of forgotten sins at the Day of Judgment.

She sank into a chair, pallid with consternation, and sat with the bill in her lap, turning the pages listlessly, and staring at the figures.

'It cannot be so much,' she cried to herself. 'It must be added up wrong;' and then she feebly tried to cast up a column; but arithmetic not being one of those accomplishments which Lady Maulevrier deemed necessary to a patrician beauty's success in life, Lesbia's education had been somewhat neglected upon this point, and she flung the bill from her in a rage, unable to hold the figures in her brain.

She opened the second envelope, her jeweller's account. At the very first item she gave another scream, fainter than the first, for her mind was getting hardened against such shocks.

'To resetting a suite of amethysts, with forty-four finest Brazilian brilliants, three hundred and fifteen pounds.'

Then followed the trifles she had bought at different visits to the shop—casual purchases, bought on the impulse of the moment. These swelled the account to a little over eight hundred pounds. Lesbia sat like a statue, numbed by despair, appalled at the idea of owing over two thousand pounds.

CHAPTER XII.

LADY LESBIA ate no luncheon that day. She went to her own room and had a cup of tea to steady her nerves, and sent to ask Lady Kirkbank to go to her as soon as she had finished luncheon. Lady Kirkbank's luncheon was a serious business, a substantial leisurely meal with which she fortified herself for the day's work. It enabled her to endure all the fatigues of visits and park, and to be airily indifferent to the charms of dinner: for Lady Kirkbank was not one of those matrons who with advanced years take to *gourmandise* as a kind of fine art. She gave good dinners, because she knew people would not come to Arlington Street to eat bad ones; but she was not a person who lived only to dine. At luncheon she gave her healthy appetite full scope, and ate like a ploughman.

She found Lesbia in her white muslin dressing gown, with cheeks as pale as the gown she wore. She was sitting in an easy chair, with a low tea-table at her side, and the two bills were in the tray among the tea-things.

'Have you any idea how much I owe Seraphine and Cabochon?' she asked, looking up despairingly at Lady Kirkbank.

'What, have they sent in their bills already?'

'Already! I wish they had sent them before. I should have known how deeply I was getting into debt.'

'Are they very heavy?'

'They are dreadful! I owe over two thousand pounds. How can I tell Lady Maulevrier that? Two thousand one hundred pounds! It is awful.'

'There are women in London who would think very little of owing twice as much,' said Lady Kirkbank, in a comforting tone, though the fact, seriously considered, could hardly afford comfort. 'Your grandmother said you were to have *carte blanche*. She may think that you have been just a little extravagant; but she can hardly be angry with you for having taken her at her word. Two thousand pounds! Yes, it certainly *is* rather stiff.'

'Seraphine is a cheat!' exclaimed Lesbia, angrily. 'Her prices are positively exorbitant!'

'My dear child, you must not say that. Seraphine is positively moderate in comparison with the new people.'

'And Mr. Cabochon, too. The idea of his charging me three hundred guineas for re-setting those stupid old amethysts.'

'My dear, you *would* have diamonds mixed with them,' said Lady Kirkbank, reproachfully.

Lesbia turned away her head with an impatient sigh. She remembered perfectly that it was Lady Kirkbank who had persuaded her to order the diamond setting; but there was no use in talking about it now. The thing was done. She was two thousand pounds in debt—two thousand pounds to these two people only — and there were ever so many shops at which she had accounts—glovers, bootmakers, habit-makers, the tailor who made her Newmarket coats and cloth gowns, the stationer who supplied her with note-paper of every variety, monogrammed, floral, sporting, illuminated with this or that device, the follies of the passing hour, hatched by penniless Invention in a garret, pandering to the vanities of the idle.

'I must write to my grandmother by this afternoon's post,' said Lesbia, with a heavy sigh.

'Impossible. We have to be at the Ranelagh by four o'clock. Smithson and some other men are to meet us there. I have promised to drive Mrs. Mostyn down. You had better begin to dress.'

'But I ought to write to-day. I had better ask for this money at once, and have done with it. Two thousand pounds! I feel as if I were a thief. You say my grandmother is not a rich woman?'

'Not rich, as the world goes nowadays. Nobody is rich now, except your commercial magnates, like Smithson. Great peers, unless their money is in London ground-rents, are great paupers. To own land is to be destitute. I don't suppose two thousand pounds will break your grandmother's bank : but of course it is a large sum to ask for at the end of two months; especially as she sent you a good deal of money while we were at Cannes. If you were engaged —about to make a really good match—you could ask for the money as a matter of course; but as it is, although you have been tremendously admired, from a practical point of view you are a failure.'

A failure. It was a hard word, but Lesbia felt it was true. She, the reigning beauty, the cynosure of every eye, had made no conquest worth talking about, except Mr. Smithson.

'Don't tell your grandmother anything about the bills for a week or two,' said Lady Kirkbank, soothingly. 'The creatures can wait for their money. Give yourself time to think.'

'I will,' answered Lesbia, dolefully.

'And now make haste, and get ready for the Ranelagh. My love, your eyes are dreadfully heavy. You *must* use a little belladonna. I'll send Rilboche to you.'

And for the first time in her life, Lesbia, too depressed to argue the point, consented to have her eyes doctored by Rilboche.

She was gay enough at the Ranelagh, and looked her loveliest at a dinner party that evening, and went to three parties after the dinner, and went home in the faint light of early morning, after sitting out a late waltz in a balcony with Mr. Smithson, a balcony banked round with hot-house flowers which were beginning to droop a little in the chilly morning air, just as beauty drooped under the searching eye of day.

Lesbia put the bills in her desk, and gave herself time to think, as Lady Kirkbank advised her. But the thinking process resulted in very little good. All the thought of which she was capable would not reduce the totals of those two dreadful accounts. And every day brought some fresh bill. The stationer, the bootmaker, the glover, the perfumer, people who had courted Lady Lesbia's custom with an air which implied that the honour of serving fashionable beauty was the first consideration, and the question of payment quite a minor point—these now began to ask for their money in the most prosaic way. Every straw added to Lesbia's burden; and her heart grew heavier with every post.

'One can see the season is waning when these people begin to pester with their accounts,' said Lady Kirkbank, who always talked of tradesmen as if they were her natural enemies.

Lesbia accepted this explanation of the avalanche of bills, and never suspected Lady Kirkbank's influence in the matter. It happened, however, that the chaperon, having her own reasons for wishing to bring Mr. Smithson's suit to a successful issue, had told Seraphine and the other people to send in their bills immediately. Lady Lesbia would be leaving London in a week or so, she informed these purveyors, and would like to settle everything before she went away.

Mr. Smithson appeared in Arlington Street almost every day, and was full of schemes for new pleasures—or pleasures as nearly new as the world of fashion can 'afford. He was particularly desirous that Sir George and Lady Kirkbank, with Lady Lesbia, should stay at his Berkshire place during the Henley week. He had a large steam launch, and the regatta was a kind of carnival for his intimate friends, who were not too proud to riot and batten upon the Parvenu's luxurious hospitality, albeit they were apt to talk somewhat slightingly of his antecedents.

Lady Kirkbank felt that this invitation was a turning point, and that if Lesbia went to stay at Rood Hall, her acceptance of Mr. Smithson was a certainty. She would see him at his place in Berkshire in the most flattering aspect; his surroundings as lord of the manor, and owner of one of the finest old places in the county, would lend dignity to his insignificance. Lesbia at first expressed a strong disinclination to go to Rood Hall. There would be a most unpleasant feeling in stopping at the house of a man whom she had refused, she told Lady Kirkbank.

'My dear, Mr. Smithson has forgiven you,' answered her chaperon. 'He is the soul of good-nature.'

'One would think he was accustomed to be refused,' said Lesbia. 'I don't want to go to Rood Hall, but I don't want to spoil your Henley week. Could not I run down to Grasmere for a week, with Kibble to take care of me, and see dear grandmother? I could tell her about those dreadful bills.'

'Bury yourself at Grasmere in the height of the season! Not to be thought of! Besides, Lady Maulevrier objected before to the idea of your travelling alone with Kibble. No! if you can't make up your mind to go to Rood Hall, George and I must make up our minds to stay away. But it will be rather hard lines; for that Henley week is quite the jolliest thing in the summer.'

'Then I'll go,' said Lesbia, with a resigned air. 'Not for worlds would I deprive you and Sir George of a pleasure.'

In her heart of hearts she rather wished to see Rood Hall. She was curious to behold the extent and magnitude of Mr. Smithson's possessions. She had seen his Italian villa in Park Lane, the perfection of modern art, modern skill, modern taste, reviving the old eternally beautiful forms, re-creating the Pitti Palace—the homes of the Medici—the halls of dead and gone Doges —and now she was told that Rood Hall—a genuine old English manor-house, in perfect preservation—was even more interesting than the villa in Park Lane. At Rood Hall there were ideal stables and farm, hot-houses without number, rose gardens, lawns, the river, and a deer park.

So the invitation was accepted, and Mr. Smithson immediately laid himself at Lesbia's feet, as it were, with regard to all other invitations for the Henley festival. Whom should he ask to meet her?—whom would she have?

‘You are very good,’ she said, ‘but I have really no wish to be consulted. I am not a Royal personage, remember. I could not presume to dictate.’

‘But I wish you to dictate. I wish you to be imperious in the expression of your wishes.’

‘Lady Kirkbank has a better right than I, if anybody is to be consulted,’ said Lesbia modestly.

Lady Kirkbank is an old dear, who gets on delightfully with everybody. But you are more sensitive. Your comfort might be marred by an obnoxious presence. I will ask nobody whom you do not like—who is not thoroughly *simpatico*. Have you no particular friends of your own choosing whom you would like me to ask?'

Lesbia confessed that she had no such friends. She liked everybody tolerably; but she had not a talent for friendship. Perhaps it was because in the London season one was too busy to make friends.

'I can fancy two girls getting quite attached to each other, out of the season,' she said, 'but in May and June life is all a rush and a scramble ——'

'And one has no time to gather wayside flowers of friendship,' interjected Mr. Smithson. 'Still, if there are no people for whom you have an especial liking, there *must* be people whom you detest.'

Lesbia owned that it was so. Detestation came of itself, naturally.

'Then let me be sure I do not ask any of your pet aversions,' said Mr. Smithson. 'You met Mr. Plantagenet Parsons, the theatrical critic, at my house. Shall we have him?'

'I like all amusing people.'

'And Horace Meander, the poet. Shall we have him? He is brimful of conceits and affectations, but he's a tremendous joke.'

'Mr. Meander is charming.'

'Suppose we ask Mostyn and his wife? Her scraps of science are rather good fun.'

'I haven't the faintest objection to the Mostyns,' replied Lesbia. 'But who are "we"?'

'We are you and I, for the nonce. The invitations will be issued ostensibly by me, but they will really emanate from you.'

'I am to be the shadow behind the throne,' said Lesbia. 'How delightful!'

'I would rather you were the sovereign ruler, on the throne,' answered Smithson, tenderly. 'That throne shall be empty till you fill it.'

'Please go on with your list of people,' said Lesbia, checking this gush of sentiment.

She began to feel somehow that she was drifting from all her moorings, that in accepting this invitation to Rood Hall she was allowing herself to be ensnared into an alliance about which she was still doubtful. If anything better had appeared in the prospect of her life—if any worthier suitor had come forward, she would have whistled Mr. Smithson down the wind; but no worthier suitor had offered himself. It was Smithson or nothing. If she did not accept Smithson, she would go back to Fellside heavily burdened with debt, and an obvious failure. She would have run the gauntlet of a London season without definite result; and this, to a young woman so impressed with her own transcendent merits, was a most humiliating state of things.

Other people's names were suggested by Mr. Smithson and approved by Lesbia, and a house-party of about fourteen in all was made up. Mr. Smithson's steam launch would comfortably accommodate that number. He had a couple of barges for chance visitors, and kept an open table on board them during the regatta.

The visit arranged, the next question was gowns. Lesbia had gowns enough to have stocked a draper's shop; but then, as she and Lady Kirkbank deplored, the difficulty was that she had worn them all, some as many as three or four times. They were doubtless all marked and known. Some of them had been described in the society papers. At Henley she would be expected to wear something distinctly new, to introduce some new fashion of gown or hat or parasol. No matter how ugly the new thing might be, so long as it was startling; no matter how eccentric, provided it was original.

'What am I to do? asked Lesbia, despairingly.

'There is only one thing that can be done. We must go instantly to Seraphine and insist upon her inventing something. If she has no idea ready she must telegraph to Worth and get him to send something over. Your old things will do very well for Rood Hall. You have no end of pretty gowns for morning and evening; but you must be original on the race days. Your gowns will be in all the papers.'

'But I shall be only getting deeper into debt,' said Lesbia, with a sigh.

'That can't be helped. If you go into society

you must be properly dressed. We'll go to Clanricarde Place directly after luncheon, and see what that old harpy has to show us.'

Lesbia had a rather uncomfortable feeling about facing the fair Seraphine, without being able to give her a cheque upon account of that dreadful bill. She had quite accepted Lady Kirkbank's idea that bills need never be discharged in full, and that the true system of finance was to give an occasional cheque on account, as a sop to Cerberus. True, that while Cerberus fattened on the sops the bill seemed always growing; and the final crash, when Cerberus grew savage and sops could be no more accepted, was too awful to be thought about.

Lesbia entered Seraphine's Louis-seize drawing-room with a faint expectation of unpleasantness; but after a little whispering between Lady Kirkbank and the dressmaker, the latter came to Lesbia smiling graciously, and seemingly full of eagerness for new orders.

'Miladi says you want something of the most original—*tant soit peu risqué*—for 'Enley,' she said. 'Let us see now,' and she tapped her forehead with a gold thimble which nobody had ever seen her use, but which looked respectable. 'There is ze dresses what Chaumont wear in zis new play, *Une Faute dans le Passé*. Yes, zere is ze watare dress—a boating party at Bougival, a toilet of the most new, striking, *écrasant*, what you English call a "screamer."'

'What a genius you are, Fifine,' exclaimed Lady Kirkbank, rapturously. 'The *Faute dans le Passé* was only produced last week. No one will have thought of reproducing Chaumont's gowns yet awhile. The idea is an inspiration.'

'What is the boating costume like?' asked Lady Lesbia, faintly.

'An exquisite combination of simplicity with *élan*,' answered the dressmaker. 'A skin-tight indigo silk Jersey bodice, closely studded with dark blue beads, a flounced petticoat of indigo and amber foulard, an amber scarf drawn tightly round the hips, and a dark blue toque with a large bunch of amber poppies. Tan-coloured mousquetaire gloves, and Hessian boots of tan-coloured kid.'

'Hessian boots!' ejaculated Lesbia.

'But, yes, Miladi. The petticoat is somewhat short, you comprehend, to escape the damp of the deck, and, after all, Hessians are much less indelicate than silk stockings, legs *à cru*, as one may say.'

'Lesbia, you will look enchanting in yellow Hessians,' said Lady Kirkbank. 'Let the dress be put in hand instantly, Seraphine.'

Lesbia was inclined to remonstrate. She did not admire the description of the costume, she would rather have something less outrageous.

'Outrageous! It is only original,' exclaimed her chaperon. 'If Chaumont wears it you may be sure it is perfect.'

'But on the stage, by gaslight, in the midst of unrealities,' argued Lesbia. 'That makes such a difference.'

'My dear, there is no difference nowadays between the stage and the drawing-room. Whatever Chaumont wears you may wear. And now let us think of the second day. I think as your first costume is to be nautical, and rather mas-

culine, your second should be somewhat languish-
ing **and** *vaporeux*. Creamy Indian muslin, **wild**
flowers, a large Leghorn hat.'

'And what will Miladi herself wear ?' asked
the French **woman of** Lady Kirkbank.   'She
must have something **of** new.'

'**No, at my** age, **it** doesn't **matter.   I** shall
wear **one of my** cotton frocks, and my Dunsta-
ble hat.'

Lesbia shuddered, for Lady Kirkbank in her
cotton frock **was a** spectacle **at which** youth
laughed and **age** blushed. **But** after **all** it did
not matter to Lesbia.   **She** would have liked a
less rowdy chaperon ; **but as a** foil **to her** own
fresh **young** beauty Lady Kirkbank **was** admirable.

They **drove down** to Rood **Hall early** next
week, Sir George conveying them in his drag,
with a change **of** horses at Maidenhead. **The**
weather was peerless ; **the** country exquisite,
approached from London. **How** different **that**
river landscape looks **to the eyes of the** traveller
returning **from the wild West of England, the**

wooded gorges of Cornwall and Devon, the Tamar and the Dart. Then how small and poor and mean seems silvery Thames, gliding peacefully between his willowy bank, singing his lullaby to the whispering sedges; a poor little river, a flat commonplace landscape, says the traveller, fresh from moorland and tor, from the rocky shore of the Atlantic, the deep clefts of the great red hills.

To Lesbia's eyes the placid stream and the green pastures, breathing odours of meadow-sweet and clover, seemed passing lovely. She was pleased with her own hat and parasol too, which made her graciously disposed towards the land-scape; and the last packet of gloves from North Audley Street fitted without a wrinkle. The glove-maker was beginning to understand her hand, which was a study for a sculptor, but which had its little peculiarities.

Nor was she ill-disposed to Mr. Smithson, who had come up to town by an early train, in order to lunch in Arlington Street and go back by coach, seated just behind Lady Lesbia, who had the box seat beside Sir George.

The drive was delightful. It was a few minutes after five when the coach drove past the picturesque old gate-house into Mr. Smithson's Park, and Rood Hall lay on the low ground in front of them, with its back to the river. It was an old red brick house, in the Tudor style, with an advanced porch, and four projecting wings, three stories high, with picturesque spire roofs overtopping the main building. Around the house ran a boldly-carved stone parapet, bearing the herons and bulrushes which were the cognisance of the noble race for which the mansion was built. Numerous projecting mullioned windows broke up the line of the park front. Lesbia was fain to own that Rood Hall was even better than Park Lane. In London Mr. Smithson had created a palace; but it was a new palace, which still had a faint flavour of bricks and mortar, and which was apt to remind the spectator of that wonderful erection of Aladdin, the famous Parvenu of Eastern story. Here, in Berkshire, Mr. Smithson had dropped into a nest which had been kept warm for him for three centuries, aired and beautified by generations of a noble race which had obligingly decayed and dwindled in order to make room for Mr. Smithson. Here the Parvenu had bought a home mellowed by the slow growth of years, touched into poetic beauty by the chastening fingers of time. His artist friends told him that every brick in the red walls was ' precious,' a mystery of colour which only a painter could fitly understand and value. Here he had bought associations, he had bought history. He had bought the dust of Elizabeth's senators, the bones of her court beauties. The coffins in the Mausoleum yonder in the ferny depths of the Park, the village church just outside the gates—these had all gone with the property.

Lesbia went up the grand staircase, through the long corridors, in a dream of wonder. Brought up at Fellside, in that new part of the Westmoreland house which had been built by her grandmother and had no history, she felt thrilled by the sober splendour of this fine old manorial mansion. All was sound and substantial, as if created yesterday, so well preserved had been the goods and chattels of the noble race; and yet all wore such unmistakeable marks of age. The deep rich colouring of the wainscot, the faded hues of the tapestry, the draperies of costliest velvet and brocade, were all sobered by the passing of years.

Mr. Smithson had shown his good taste in having kept all things as Sir Hubert Heronville, the last of his race, had left them; and the Heronvilles had been one of those grand old Tory races which change nothing of the past.

Lady Lesbia's bedroom was the State chamber, which had been occupied by kings and queens in days of yore. That grandiose four-poster, with the carved ebony columns, cut velvet curtains, and plumes of ostrich feathers, had been built for Elizabeth, when she deigned to include Rood Hall in one of her royal progresses. Charles the First had rested his weary head upon those very pillows, before he went on to the Inn at Uxbridge, where he was to be lodged less luxuriously. James the Second had stayed there when Duke of York, with Mistress Anne Hyde, before he acknowledged his marriage to the multitude; and Anne's daughter had occupied the same room as Queen of England forty years later; and now the Royal chamber, with adjacent dressing-room, and oratory, and spacious boudoir all in the same suite, was reserved for Lady Lesbia Haselden.

'I'm afraid you are spoiling me,' she told Mr. Smithson, when he asked if she approved of the rooms that had been allotted to her. 'I feel quite ashamed of myself among the ghosts of dead and gone queens.'

'Why so? Surely the Royalty of beauty has as divine a right as that of an anointed sovereign.'

'I hope the Royal personages don't walk,' exclaimed Lady Kirkbank, in her girlish tone: 'this is just the house in which one would expect ghosts.'

Whereupon Mrs. Mostyn hastened to enlighten the company upon the real causes of ghost-seeing, which she had lately studied in Carpenter's 'Mental Physiology,' and favoured them with a diluted version of the views of that authority.

This was at afternoon tea in the library, where the brass-wired bookcases, filled with mighty folios and handsome octavos in old bindings, looked as if they had not been opened for a century. The literature of past ages furnished the room, and made a delightful background. The literature of the present lay about on the tables, and testified that the highest intellectual flight of the inhabitants of Rood Hall was a dip into the *Contemporary* or the *Nineteenth Century*, or the perusal of the last new scandal in the shape of Reminiscences, or Autobiography. One large round table was consecrated to Mudie, another to Rolandi. On the one side you had Mrs. Oliphant on the other Zola, exemplifying the genius of the two nations.

After tea Mr. Smithson's visitors, most of whom had arrived in Sir George's drag, explored the grounds. These were lovely beyond expression in the low afternoon light. Cedars of Lebanon spread their broad shadows on the velvet lawn, yews and Wellingtonias of mighty growth made an atmosphere of gloom in some parts of the

grounds. One great feature was the Ladies
Garden, a spot apart, a great square garden
surrounded with a laurel wall, eight feet high,
containing a rose garden, where the choicest
specimens grew and flourished, while in the
centre there was a circular fish-pond with a
fountain. There was a Lavender Walk too,
another feature of the grounds at Rood Hall, an
avenue of tall lavender bushes, much affected by
the stately dames of old.

Modern manners preferred the river terrace, as
a pleasant place on which to loiter after dinner,
to watch the boats flashing by in the evening
light, or the sun going down behind a fringe of
willows on the opposite bank. This Italian terrace, with its statues, and carved vases filled with
roses, fuchsias, and geraniums, was the great point
of rendezvous at Rood Hall—an ideal spot whereon
to linger in the deepening twilight, from which
to gaze upon the moonlit river later on in the
night.

The windows of the drawing-room, and music-
room, and ball-room opened on to this terrace,

and the royal wing — the tower-shaped wing now devoted to Lady Lesbia, looked upon the terrace and the river.

'Lovely as your house is altogether, I think this river view is the best part of it,' said Lady Lesbia, as she strolled with Mr. Smithson on the terrace after dinner, dressed in Indian muslin which was almost as poetical as a vapour, and with a cloud of delicate lace wrapped round her head. 'I think I shall spend half of my life at my boudoir window, gloating over that delicious landscape.'

Horace Meander, the poet, was discoursing to a select group upon that peculiar quality of willows which causes them to shiver, and quiver, and throw little lights and shadows on the river, and on the subtle, ineffable beauty of twilight, which, perhaps, however utterly beautiful in the abstract, would have been more agreeable to him personally if he had not been surrounded by a cloud of gnats, which refused to be buffeted off his laurel-crowned head.

While Mr. Meander poetised in his usual eloquent style, Mrs. Mostyn, as a still newer light, discoursed as eloquently to a little knot of women, imparting valuable information upon the anatomical structure and individual peculiarities of those various insects which are the pests of a summer evening.

'You don't like gnats!' exclaimed the lady; 'how very extraordinary. Do you know I have spent days and weeks upon the study of their habits and dear little ways. They are the most interesting creatures—far superior to *us* in intellect. Do you know that they fight, and that they have tribes which are life-long enemies—like those dreadful Corsicans—and that they make little sepulchres in the bark of trees, and bury each other—alive, if they can; and they hold vestries, and have burial boards. They are most absorbing creatures, if you only give yourself up to the study of them; but it is no use to be half-hearted in a study of that kind. I went without so much as a cup of tea for twenty-four hours, watching my gnats, for fear the opening of the door should startle them. Another time I shall make the nursery governess watch for me.'

'How interesting, how noble of you,' exclaimed

the other ladies; and then they began to talk about bonnets, **and** about Mr. Smithson, to speculate how much money this house and all his other houses had cost him, and to wonder if he was really rich, or if **he** were only one **of** those great financial windbags which so often explode and leave **the** world aghast, marvelling at the ease with which it has been deluded.

They wondered, too, whether Lady Lesbia Haselden meant to marry him.

'Of course she does, my dear,' answered Mrs. Mostyn, decisively. 'You don't suppose that after having studied **the** habits of *gnats* I cannot read such a poor shallow creature as a silly vain girl. Of **course** Lady Lesbia means to marry Mr. Smithson's fine houses; and she is only amusing herself and swelling her own importance **by** letting him dangle **in** a kind of suspense which is not suspense; for he knows as well as she does that she means **to** have him.'

The next day was given up, first to seeing the house, an amusement which lasted very well for an hour or so after breakfast, and then to wandering in a desultory manner, to rowing and canoeing, and a little sailing, and a good deal of screaming and pretty timidity upon the blue bright river; to gathering wild flowers and ferns in rustic lanes, and to an *al fresco* luncheon in the wood at Medmenham, and then dinner, and then music, an evening spent half within and half without the music-room, cigarettes sparkling like glowworms on the terrace, tall talk from Mr. Meander, long quotations from his own muse and that of Rossetti, a little Shelley, a little Keats, a good deal of Swinburne. The festivities were late on this second evening, as Mr. Smithson had invited a good many people from the neighbourhood, but the house party were not the less early on the following morning, which was the first Henley day.

It was a peerless morning, and all the brass-work of Mr. Smithson's launch sparkled and shone in the sun as she lay in front of the terrace. A wooden pier, a portable construction, was thrown out from the terrace steps, to enable the company to go on board the launch without the possibility of wet feet or damaged raiment.

Lesbia's Chamount costume was a success. The women praised it, the men stared and admired. The dark-blue silken jersey, sparkling with closely studded indigo beads, fitted the slim graceful figure as a serpent's scales fit the serpent. The coquettish little blue silk toque, the careless cluster of gold-coloured poppies, against the glossy brown hair, the large sunshade of old gold satin lined with indigo, the flounced petticoat of softest Indian silk, the dainty little tan-coloured boots with high heels and pointed toes, were all perfect after their fashion ; and Mr. Smithson felt that the liege lady of his life, the woman he meant to marry willy nilly would be the belle of the racecourse. Nor was he disappointed. Everybody in London had heard of Lady Lesbia Haselden. Her photograph was in all the West End windows, was enshrined in the albums of South Kensington and Clapham, Maida Vale and Haverstock Hill. People whose circles were far remote from Lady Lesbia's circle were as familiar with her beauty as if they had known her from her cradle. And all these outsiders wanted to see her in the flesh, just as they always thirst to behold Royal personages. So when it became known that the beautiful Lady Lesbia Haselden was on board Mr. Smithson's launch, all the people in the small boats, or on neighbouring barges, made it their business to have a good look at her. The launch was almost mobbed by those inquisitive little boats in the intervals between the races.

'What are the people all staring and hustling one another for ?' asked Lesbia, innocently. She had seen the same hustling and whispering and staring in the hall at the opera, when she was waiting for her carriage ; but she chose to affect unconsciousness. 'What do they all want ? '

'I think they want to see you,' said Mr. Smithson, who was sitting by her side. 'A very natural desire.'

Lesbia laughed, and lowered the big yellow sunshade, so as to hide herself altogether from the starers.

'How silly!' she exclaimed. 'It is all the fault of those horrid photographers : they vulgarise everything and everybody. I will never be photographed again.'

'Oh yes, you will, and in that frock. It's the prettiest thing I've seen for a long time. Why do you hide yourself from those poor wretches, who keep rowing backwards and forwards in an obviously aimless way, just to get a peep at you *en passant?* What happiness for us who live near you, and can gaze when we will, without all those absurd manœuvres. There goes the signal—and now for a hard-fought race.'

Lesbia pretended to be interested in the racing—she pretended to be gay, but her heart was as heavy as lead. That burden of debt, which had been growing ever since Seraphine sent in her bill, was weighing her down to the dust.

She owed three thousand pounds. It seemed incredible that she should owe so much, that a girl's frivolous fancies and extravagances could amount to such a sum within so short a span. But thoughtless purchases, ignorant orders, had run on from week to week, and the main result was an indebtedness of close upon three thousand pounds.

Three thousand pounds ! The sum was continually sounding in her ears like the cry of a screech owl. The very ripple of the river flowing so peacefully under the blue summer sky seemed to repeat the words. Three thousand pounds! 'Is it much?' she wondered, having no standard of comparison. 'Is it very much more than my grandmother will expect me to have spent in the time? Will it trouble her to have to pay those bills? Will she be very angry?'

These were questions which Lesbia kept asking herself, in every pause of her frivolous existence; in such a pause as this, for instance, while the people round her were standing breathless, open-mouthed, gazing after the boats. She did not care a straw for the boats, who won, or who lost the race. It was all a hollow mockery. Indeed it seemed just now that the only real thing in life was those accursed bills, which would have to be paid somehow.

She had told Lady Maulevrier nothing about them as yet. She had allowed herself to be advised by Lady Kirkbank, and she had taken time to think. But thought had given her no help. The days were gliding onward, and Lady Maulevrier would have to be told.

She meditated perplexedly about her grandmother's income. She had never heard the extent of it, but had taken for granted that Lady Maulevrier was rich. Would three thousand pounds make a great inroad on that income? Would it be a year's income?—half a year's? Lesbia had no idea. Life at Fellside was carried on in an elegant manner—with considerable luxury in house and garden—a luxury of flowers, a lavish expenditure of labour. Yet the expenditure of Lady Maulevrier's existence, spent always on the same spot, must be as nothing to the money spent in such a life as Lady Kirkbank's, which involved the keeping up of three or four houses, and costly journeys to and fro, and incessant change of attire.

No doubt Lady Maulevrier had saved money; yes, she must have saved thousands during her long seclusion, Lesbia argued. Her grandmother had told her that she was to look upon herself as an heiress. This could only mean that Lady

Maulevrier had a fortune to leave her; and this being so, what could it matter if she had anticipated some of her portion? And yet, and yet there was in her heart of hearts a terrible fear of that stern dowager, of the cold scorn in those splendid eyes when she should stand revealed in all her foolishness, her selfish, mindless, vain extravagances. She, who had never been reproved, shrank with a sickly dread from the idea of reproof. And to be told that her career as a fashionable beauty had been a failure! That would be the bitterest pang of all.

Soon came luncheon, and Heidseck, and then an afternoon which was gayer than the morning had been, inasmuch as every one babbled and laughed more after luncheon. And then there was five o'clock tea on deck, under the striped Japanese awning, to the jingle of banjos, enlivened by the wit of black-faced minstrels, amidst wherries and canoes and gondolas, and ponderous house-boats, and snorting launches, crowding the sides of the sunlit river, in full view of the crowd yonder in front of the Red Lion, and here on this nearer bank, and all along either shore, fringing the green meadows with a gaudy border of smartly-dressed humanity.

It was a gay scene, and Lesbia gave herself up to the amusement of the hour, and talked and chaffed as she had learned to talk and chaff in one brief season, holding her own against all comers.

Rood Hall looked lovely when they went back to it in the gloaming, an Elizabethan pile crowned with towers. The four wings with their conical roofs, the massive projecting windows, grey stone, ruddy brickwork, lattices reflecting the sunlight, Italian terrace and blue river in the foreground, cedars and yews at the back, all made a splendid picture of an English ancestral home.

'Nice old place, isn't it?' asked Mr. Smithson, seeing Lesbia's admiring gaze as the launch neared the terrace. They two were standing in the bows, apart from all the rest.

'Nice! it is simply perfect.'

'Oh no it isn't. There is one thing wanted yet.'

'What is that?'

'A wife. You are the only person who can make any house of mine perfect. Will you?' He took her hand, which she did not withdraw from his grasp. He bent his head and kissed the little hand in its soft Swedish glove.

'Will you, Lesbia?' he repeated earnestly; and she answered softly, 'Yes.'

That one brief syllable was more like a sigh than a spoken word, and it seemed to her as if in the utterance of that syllable the three thousand pounds had been paid.

CHAPTER XIII.

'KIND IS MY LOVE TO-DAY, TO-MORROW KIND.'

WHILE Lady Lesbia was draining the cup of
London folly and London care to the dregs, Lady
Mary was leading her usual quiet life beside the
glassy lake, where the green hill-sides and sheep
walks were reflected in all their summer verdure
under the cloudless azure of a summer sky. A
monotonous life—passing dull as seen from the
outside—and yet Mary was very happy, happy
even in her solitude, with the grave deep joy of a
satisfied heart, a mind at rest. All life had taken
a new colour since her engagement to John Hammond. A sense of new duties, an awakening
earnestness had given a graver tone to her character.
Her spirits were less wild, yet not less joyous
than of old. The joy was holier, deeper.

Her lover's letters were the chief delight of

her lonely days. To read them again and again, and ponder upon them, and then to pour out all her heart and mind in answering them. These were pleasures enough for her young life. Hammond's letters were such as any woman might be proud to receive. They were not love-letters only. He wrote as friend to friend; not descending from the proud pinnacle of masculine intelligence to the lower level of feminine silliness; not writing down to a simple country girl's capacity; but writing fully and fervently, as if there were no subject too lofty or too grave for the understanding of his betrothed. He wrote as one sure of being sympathised with, wrote as to his second self: and Mary showed herself not unworthy of the honour thus rendered to her intellect.

There was one world which had newly opened to Mary since her engagement, and that was the world of politics. Hammond had told her that his ambition was to succeed as a politician—to do some good in his day as one of the governing body; and of late she had made it her business to learn how England and the world outside England were governed.

She had no natural leaning to the study of political economy. Indeed, she had always imagined any question relating to the government of her country to be inherently dry-as-dust and uninviting. But had John Hammond devoted his days to the study of Coptic manuscripts, or the arrow-headed inscriptions upon Assyrian tablets, she would have toiled her hardest in the endeavour to make herself a Coptic scholar, or an adept in the cuneiform characters. If he had been a student of Chinese, she would not have been discomfited by such a trifle as the fifty thousand characters in the Chinese alphabet.

And so, as he was to make his name in the arena of public life, she set herself to acquire a proper understanding of the science of politics; and to this end she gorged herself with English history,—Hume, Hallam, Green, Justin McCarthy, Palgrave, Lecky, from the days of Witenagemote to the Reform Bill; the Repeal of the Corn Laws, the Disestablishment of the Irish Church, Ballot, Trade

Unionism, and unreciprocated Free Trade. No question was deep enough to repel her; for was not her lover interested in the dryest thereof? and what concerned him and his welfare must needs be full of interest for her.

To this end she read the debates religiously day by day; and she one day ventured shyly to suggest that she should read them aloud to Lady Maulevrier.

'Would it not be a little rest for you if I were to read your 'Times' aloud to you every afternoon, grandmother?' she asked. 'You read so many books, French, English, and German, and I think your eyes must get a little tired sometimes.'

Mary ventured the remark with some timidity, for those falcon eyes were fixed upon her all the time, bright and clear and steady as the eyes of youth. It seemed almost an impertinence to suggest that such eyes could know weariness.

'No, Mary, my sight holds out wonderfully for an old woman,' replied her ladyship, gently. 'The new theory of the last oculist whose book

I dipped into—a very amusing and interesting book, by-the-bye—is that the sight improves and strengthens by constant use, and that an agricultural labourer, who hardly uses his eyes at all, has rarely in the decline of life so good a sight as the watchmaker or the student. I have read immensely all my life, and find myself no worse for that indulgence. But you may read the debates to me if you like, my dear, for if my eyes are strong, I myself am very tired. Sick to death, Mary, sick to death.'

The splendid eyes turned from Mary, and looked away to the blue sky, to the hills in their ineffable beauty of colour and light — shifting, changing with every moment of the summer day. Intense weariness, a settled despair, were expressed in that look—tearless, yet sadder than all tears.

'It must be very monotonous, very sad for you,' murmured Mary, her own eyes brimming over with tears. 'But it will not be always so, dear grandmother. I hope a time will come when you will be able to go about again, to resume your old life.'

'I do not hope, Mary. No, child, I feel and know that time will never come. My strength is ebbing slowly day by day. If I live for another year, live to see Lesbia married, and you, too, perhaps—well, I shall die at peace. At peace, no; not——' She faltered, and the thin, semi-transparent hand was pressed upon her brow. 'What will be said of me when I am dead?'

Mary feared that her grandmother's mind was wandering. She came and knelt beside the couch, and laid her head against the satin pillows, tenderly, caressingly.

'Dear grandmother, pray be calm,' she murmured.

'Mary, do not look at me like that, as if you would read my heart. There are hearts that must not be looked into. Mine is like a charnel-house. Monotonous, yes; my life has been monotonous. No conventual gloom was ever deeper than the gloom of Fellside. My boy did nothing to lighten it for me, and his son followed in his father's footsteps. You and Lesbia have been my only consolation. Lesbia!

I was so proud of her beauty, so proud and fond of her, because she was like me, and recalled my own youth. And see how easily she forgets me. She has gone into a new world, in which my age and my infirmities have no part; and I am as nothing to her.'

Mary changed from red to pale, so painful was her embarrassment. What could she say in defence of her sister? How could she deny that Lesbia was an ingrate, when those rare and hurried letters, so careless in their tone, expressing the selfishness of the writer in every syllable, told but too plainly of forgetfulness and ingratitude?

'Dear grandmother, Lesbia has so much to do —her life is so full of engagements,' she faltered feebly.

'Yes, she goes from party to party — she gives herself up heart and mind and soul to pleasures which she ought to consider only as the trivial means to great ends; and she forgets the woman who reared her, and cared for her, and watched over her from her infancy, and who tried to inspire her with a noble ambition. —Yes, read to me, child, read. Give me new thoughts, if you can, for my brain is weary with grinding the old ones. There was a grand debate in the Lords last night, and Lord Hartfield spoke. Let me hear his speech. You can read what was said by the man before him; never mind the rest.'

Mary read Lord Somebody's speech, which was passing dull, but which prepared the ground for a magnificent and exhaustive reply from Lord Hartfield. The question was an important one, affecting the well-being of the masses, and Lord Hartfield spoke with an eloquence which rose in force and fire as he wound himself like a serpent into the heart of his subject—beginning quietly, soberly, with no opening flashes of rhetoric, but rising gradually to the topmost heights of oratory.

'What a speech!' cried Lady Maulevrier, delighted, her cheeks glowing, her eyes kindling; 'what a noble fellow the speaker must be! Oh, Mary, I must tell you a secret. I loved that man's father. Yes, my dear, I loved him fondly, dearly, truly, as you love that young man of yours ; and he was the only man I ever really loved. Fate parted us. But I have never forgotten him— never, Mary, never. At this moment I have but to close my eyes and I can see his face—see him looking at me as he looked the last time we met. He was a younger son, poor, his future quite hopeless in those days ; but it was not my fault we were parted. I would have married him—yes, wedded poverty, just as you are going to marry this Mr. Hammond ; but my people would not let me ; and I was too young, too helpless, to make a good fight. Oh, Mary, if I had only fought hard enough, what a happy woman I might have been, and how good a wife.'

'You were a good wife to my grandfather, I am sure,' faltered Mary, by way of saying something consolatory.

A dark frown came over Lady Maulevrier's face, which had softened to deepest tenderness just before.

'A good wife to Maulevrier,' she said, in a

mocking tone. 'Well, yes, as good a wife as such a husband deserved. I was better than Cæsar's wife, Mary, for no breath of suspicion ever rested upon my name. But if I had married Ronald Hollister, I should have been a happy woman; and that I have never been since I parted from him.'

'You have never seen the present Lord Hartfield, I think?'

'Never: but I have watched his career. I have thought of him. His father died while he was an infant, and he was brought up in seclusion by a widowed mother, who kept him tied to her apron-string till he went to Oxford. She idolised him, and I am told she taught herself Latin and Greek, mathematics even, in order to help him in his boyish studies, and, later on, read Greek plays and Latin poetry with him, till she became an exceptional classic for a woman. She was her son's companion and friend, sympathised with his tastes, his pleasures, his friendships; devoted every hour of her life, every thought of her mind to his welfare, his interests;

walked with him, rode with him, travelled half over Europe, yachted with him. Her friends all declared that the lad would grow up an odious milksop ; but I am told that there never was a manlier man than Lord Hartfield. From his boyhood he was his mother's protector, helped to administer her affairs, acquired a premature sense of responsibility, and escaped almost all those vices which make young men detestable. His mother died within a few months of his majority. He was broken-hearted at losing her, and left Europe immediately after her death. From that time he has been a great traveller. But I suppose now that he has taken his seat in the House of Lords, and has spoken a good many times, he means to settle down and take his place among the foremost men of his day. I am told that he is worthy to take such a place.'

' You must feel warmly interested in watching his career,' said Mary, sympathetically.

' I am interested in everything that concerns him. I will tell you another secret, Mary. I think I am getting into my dotage, my dear, or I should hardly talk to you like this,' said Lady Maulevrier, with a touch of bitterness.

Mary was sitting on a stool by the sofa, close to the invalid's pillow. She clasped her grandmother's hand and kissed it fondly.

'Dear grandmother, I think you are talking to me like this to-day because you are beginning to care for me a little,' she said, tenderly.

'Oh, my dear, you are very good, very sweet and forgiving to care for me at all, after my neglect of you,' answered Lady Maulevrier, with a sigh. 'I have kept you out in the cold so long, Mary. Lesbia—well, Lesbia has been a kind of infatuation for me, and like all infatuations mine has ended in disappointment and bitterness. Ambition has been the bane of my life, Mary ; and when I could no longer be ambitious for myself—when my own existence had become a mere death in life, I began to dream and to scheme for the aggrandisement of my granddaughter. Lesbia's beauty, Lesbia's elegance seemed to make success certain—and so I dreamt my dream—which may never be fulfilled.'

'What was your dream, grandmother? May I know all about it?'

'That was the secret I spoke of just now. Yes, Mary, you may know, for I fear the dream will never be realised. I wanted my Lesbia to become Lord Hartfield's wife. I would have brought them together myself, could I but have gone to London; but, failing that, I fancied Lady Kirkbank would have divined my wishes without being told them, and would have introduced Hartfield to Lesbia; and now the London season is drawing to a close, and Hartfield and Lesbia have never met. He hardly goes anywhere, I am told. He devotes himself exclusively to politics; and he is not in Lady Kirkbank's set. A terrible disappointment to me, Mary!'

'It is a pity,' said Mary. 'Lesbia is so lovely. If Lord Hartfield were fancy-free he ought to fall in love with her, could they but meet. I thought that in London all fashionable people knew each other, and were continually meeting.

'It used to be so in my day, Mary. Almack's

was a common ground, even if there had been no other. But now there are circles and circles, I believe, rings that touch occasionally, but never break and mingle. I am afraid poor Georgie's set is not quite so nice as I could have wished. Yet Lesbia writes as if she were in raptures with her chaperon, and with all the people she meets. And then Georgie tells me that this Mr. Smithson whom Lesbia has refused is a very important personage, a millionaire, and very likely to be made a peer.'

' A new peer,' said Mary, making a wry face. ' One would rather have an old commoner. I always fancy a newly-made peer must be like a newly-built house, glaring, and staring, and arid and uncongenial.'

' *C'est selon*,' said Lady Maulevrier. ' One would not despise a Chatham or a Wellington because of the newness of his title; but a man who has only money to recommend him ——'

Lady Maulevrier left her sentence unfinished, save by a shrug; while Mary made another wry face. She had that grand contempt for sordid wealth which is common to young people who have never known the want of money.

'I hope Lesbia will marry some one better than Mr. Smithson,' she said.

'I hope so too, dear; and yet do you know I have an idea that Lesbia means to accept Mr. Smithson, or she would hardly have consented to go to his house for the Henley week. Here is a letter from Georgie Kirkbank which you will have to answer for me to-morrow—a letter full of raptures about Mr. Smithson's place in Berkshire. Rood Hall. I remember the house well. I was there nearly fifty years ago, when the Heronvilles owned it; and now the Heronvilles are all dead or ruined, and this city person is master of the fine old mansion. It is a strange world, Mary.'

From that time forward Mary and her grand-mother were on more confidential terms, and when, two days later, Fellside was startled into life by the unexpected arrival of Lord Maulevrier and Mr. Hammond, the dowager seemed almost as pleased as her granddaughter at the arrival of the young men.

As for Mary, she was almost beside herself with joy when she heard their voices from the lawn, and, rushing to the shrubbery, saw them walk up the hill, as she had seen them on that first evening nearly a year ago, when John Hammond came as a stranger to Fellside.

She tried to take her joy soberly, though her eyes were dancing with delight, as she went to the porch to meet them.

'What extraordinary young men you are,' she said, as she emerged breathless from her lover's embrace. 'The idea of your descending upon us without a moment's notice. Why did you not write or telegraph, that your rooms might be ready?'

'Am I to understand that all the spare rooms at Fellside are kept as damp as the bottom of the lake?' asked Maulevrier. 'I did not think any preparation was necessary: but we can go back if we're not wanted, can't we, Jack?'

'You darling,' cried Mary, hanging affectionately upon her brother's arm. 'You *know* I was only joking, you *know* how enraptured I am to have you.'

'To have *me*, only me,' said Maulevrier. 'Jack doesn't count, I suppose?'

'You know how glad I am, and that I want to hide my gladness,' answered Mary, radiant and blushing like the rich red roses in the porch. 'You men are so vain. And now come and see grandmother. She will be cheered by your arrival. She has been so good to me just lately, so sweet.'

'She might have been good and sweet to you all your life,' said Hammond. 'I am not prepared to be grateful to her at a moment's notice for any crumbs of affection she may throw you.'

'Oh, but you must be grateful, sir; and you must love her and pity her,' retorted Mary. 'Think how sadly she has suffered. We cannot be too kind to her, or too fond of her, poor dear.'

'Mary is right,' said Hammond, half in jest and half in earnest. 'What wonderful instincts these young women have.'

'Come and see her ladyship; and then you must have dinner, just as you had that first evening,' said Mary. 'We'll act that first evening over again, Jack; only you can't fall in love with Lesbia, as she isn't here.'

'I don't think I surrendered that first evening, Mary. Though I thought your sister the loveliest girl I had ever seen.'

'And what did you think of me, sir? Tell me that,' said Mary.

'Shall I tell you the truth, the whole truth, and nothing but the truth?'

'Of course.'

'Then I freely confess that I did not think about you at all. You were there—a pretty, innocent, bright young maiden, with big brown eyes and auburn hair; but I thought no more about you than I did about the Gainsborough on the wall, which you very much resemble.'

'That is most humiliating,' said Mary, pouting a little in the midst of her bliss.

'No, dearest, it is only natural,' answered Hammond. 'I believe if all the happy lovers in this world could be questioned, at least half of them would confess to having thought very little about each other at first meeting. They meet, and touch hands, and part again, and never guess the mystery of the future, which wraps them round like a cloud, never say of each other, There is my fate; and then they meet again, and again, as hazard wills, and never know that they are drifting to their doom.'

Mary rang bells and gave orders, just as she had done in that summer gloaming a year ago. The young men had arrived just at the same hour, on the stroke of nine, when the eight o'clock dinner was over and done with; for a *téte-à-téte* meal with Fräulein Müller was not a feast to be prolonged on account of its felicity. Perhaps they had so contrived as to arrive exactly at this hour.

Lady Maulevrier received them both with extreme cordiality. But the young men saw a change for the worse in the invalid since the spring. The face was thinner, the eyes too bright, the flush upon the hollow cheek had a hectic tinge, the voice was feebler. Hammond was reminded of a falcon or an eagle pining and wasting in a cage.

'I am very glad to see you, Mr. Hammond,'

said Lady Maulevrier, giving him her hand, and addressing him with unwonted cordiality. 'It was a happy thought that brought you and Maulevrier here. When an old woman is as near the grave as I am her relatives ought to look after her. I shall be glad to have a little private conversation with you to-morrow, Mr. Hammond, if you can spare me a few minutes.'

'As many hours, if your ladyship pleases,' said Hammond. 'My time is entirely at your service.'

'Oh no, you will want to be roaming about the hills with Mary, discussing your plans for the future. I shall not encroach too much on your time. But I am very glad you are here.'

'We shall only trespass on you for a few days,' said Maulevrier; 'just a flying visit.'

'How is it that you are not both at Henley?' asked Mary. 'I thought all the world was at Henley.'

'Who is Henley? what is Henley?' demanded Maulevrier, pretending ignorance.

'I believe Maulevrier has lost so much money backing his college boat on previous occasions that he is glad to run away from the regatta this year,' said Hammond.

'I have a sister there,' replied his friend. 'That's an all-sufficient explanation. When a fellow's women-kind take to going to races and regattas it is high time for *him* to stop away.'

'Have you seen Lesbia lately?' asked his grandmother.

'About ten days ago.'

'And did she seem happy?'

Maulevrier shrugged his shoulders.

'She was vacillating between the refusal or the acceptance of a million of money and four or five fine houses. I don't know whether that condition of mind means happiness. I should call it an intermediate state.'

'Why do you make silly jokes about serious questions? Do you think Lesbia means to accept this Mr. Smithson?'

'All London thinks so.'

'And is he a good man?'

'Good for a hundred thousand pounds at half an hour's notice.'

'Is he worthy of your sister?'

Maulevrier paused, looked at his grandmother with a curious expression, and then replied—

'I think he is —quite.'

'Then I am content that she should marry him,' said Lady Maulevrier, 'although he is a nobody.'

'Oh, but he is a very important nobody, a nobody who can get a peerage next year, backed by the Maulevrier influence, which I suppose would count for something.'

'Most of *my* friends are dead,' said Lady Maulevrier, 'but there are a few survivors of the past who might help me.'

'I don't think there'll be any difficulty about the peerage. Smithson stumped up very handsomely at the last General Election, and the Conservatives are not strong enough to be ungrateful. "These have no master."'

END OF VOLUME II.

WILLIAM RIDER AND SON, PRINTERS, LONDON.